BLACK BLOOM

A Story of Survival

By Felix I.D. Dimaro

BLACK BLOOM

Written by FELIX I.D. DIMARO

Cover Artwork: Rosco Nischler
Interior Artwork: Zach Horvath, Janie Nischler
Typography and Graphic Design: Courtney Swank
Editor: Alessandra Sztrimbely

Copyright © 2022 by Felix I.D. Dimaro

ALSO BY FELIX I.D. DIMARO

How To Make A Monster:
The Loveliest Shade of Red

Bug Spray:
A Tale of Madness

Viral Lives:
A Ghost Story

2222

The Fire On Memory Lane

The Corruption of Philip Toles

For Earth, with many apologies

"There's so much pollution in the air now that if it weren't for our lungs there'd be no place to put it all."

- **Robert Orben**

A STORY OF SURVIVAL

By Alexander Langston

Dedicated to Eunice Jung

Written and revised between
May 3 – May 7, 2045

A Summary of Events

It was a month into spring when the first black dandelion was sighted and reported in the news. That was Saturday, April 22, 2045; only two weeks ago. Which almost feels impossible considering all that has changed since then. It was also Earth Day. The significance of the date wasn't lost upon me.

Earth Day was an occasion on par with Valentine's Day. One on which people pledged to show love to the planet as a makegood for the centuries we've treated it as though we hated it. That's not how the marketing companies pitched it, but that's what it was.

Still, despite the significance of the day, I remember thinking that the news of the black dandelions was only interesting in a distant sort of way. Like the sound of unexpected fireworks on a midsummer night, it caught my attention but not for too long, and never fully. I can't imagine many people could have thought that those little black flowers were a sign of the end of everything as we knew it. I certainly didn't think that was the case.

You never expect the worst to happen until it happens, which is what makes it the worst. That's what my wife would sometimes say. I agree with her about that. Things might not have been so bad had we been expecting it. Though I can't imagine how they might have gone much better.

It was my wife, Eunice Jung, who inspired me to name this document what it is: "A Story of Survival." It's an optimistic title, one I likely wouldn't have chosen had I not felt the need to project that optimism toward my wife as she struggled. Had she and I both been okay throughout this ordeal, I may have gone with something like "The Way It All Ended" or "The Final War." But I've never quite been the positive sort, whereas my wife exudes optimism the way most people do sweat.

Eunice was always the positive one of the two of us. She was the leader in the household and my guiding light. The moment she went blind, it felt as though I was the one in the dark.

I don't know how she does it. Constantly staying strong, even through this nightmare. But I suppose others have said the same about me, given the wheelchair I'm almost always connected to. But I'm not brave like she is. I'm not courageous. I don't know how to tell those people who assume I'm some hero because I can't walk and they can that I am simply just living. I guess she's simply living too, she just knows how to do so in a way that lets others feel as though they can live as well. That's why I love her, and that's why I'm lucky she loves me. It's our love that kept us together right until the end.

I should properly introduce myself. My name is Alexander Langston, and I write for a living. However, documenting history as it happens isn't quite my area of expertise. I hope you can forgive me if things seem a bit jumbled. Life right now seems a bit jumbled.

Let me start with the straightforward facts: I live at 2 Eaglestone Court in Daphnis, Washington, a suburb outside of Seattle. My bungalow is one of a handful of houses tucked away in a modest cul-de-sac. Most people would consider it to be a nice house. Even a bit excessive for a couple with no kids. I feel fortunate to have it every single day.

I work as a children's author. It seems so insignificant to even mention that fact now, but there was a time when that sentence meant the world to me: I work as a children's author.

The first time I was able to say that sentence was the second time my life truly changed. What's happening now is the third.

The first time my life truly changed was after the accident that put me in a wheelchair permanently, and what led to and resulted from that accident.

The accident changed a lot of things for me. Aside from losing the ability to walk, I lost the ability to dream and hope for the future. Without my legs, I had no idea what I would do.

I was twenty-two when it happened. A former high school athlete and recent college dropout, I was already lost prior to the accident. The fact that my parents had died not too long before I lost my legs made it almost impossible for me to find myself.

I spent the first year after their death adrift, only sober when I had to go to physical therapy. And because my parents had left me more than enough money to live on, I hadn't been in a rush to get my life together. I was as lost as I had ever been until these recent events with the black dandelions. It wasn't until meeting Eunice that I got back on track again. Twenty-three years later, and it was Eunice who, despite all she has been through, was keeping me from becoming unmoored, set adrift, once more.

It was her all those years ago who inspired my entire writing career. One which revolved around a series of children's books called *Freddy the Fearless Feline*. Books about a three-legged alley cat who overcame all obstacles in the rough and tumble town of Dogsville. It was really just a series of allegories for my life and my recovery, inspired by Eunice and her encouragement of me.

But I'm getting ahead of myself. And honestly, I don't know why all of these details are important. I fear that if this isn't the absolute worst, and there is something even worse to come, the people who find what is left might want as many details as possible. Sort of like how we look back at ancient cave dwellings full of etchings and paintings - people would kill to know what the cave artists did for a living when they weren't crudely drawing their cavemates and the creatures they interacted with.

Were the cave artists hunters? Gatherers? Female painters? Maybe cavemen didn't all behave like "cavemen." Maybe the women ruled the roost. Maybe cave dwelling societies paid their artists in food and shells; maybe art was all that those who etched on the walls of caves did. Maybe the artists were just a bunch of caveteens, bored and messing around.

We wonder about that kind of thing now, and I wonder if people in the future will do the same if this is the end and the world is forced to restart after what has happened over the last few weeks.

What has happened is a series of events that has forever changed the world as we know it. I hope one day, maybe years from now, some group of survivors will finally rummage through what we leave behind, hopeful to learn any and everything about the world and how it was before this, as well as during this. If this document is found, I would like for it to be as helpful to those survivors as possible.

I'm no historian, but I'll do my best to capture the spirit of the times as they were before the first black dandelion showed up and sent the world to chaos. More importantly, I hope to document how humanity has responded to the greatest challenge we have ever faced.

I think of it as the apocalypse. I know that sounds dramatic, and I know Eunice would dismiss the word "apocalypse." She would call this just another (very large) pothole in the road of life. She would remind me that both she and I have overcome potholes that would have left others stuck.

Unfortunately, Eunice went blind. Fortunately, Eunice can't see what this disease has done to her, our neighbors, and so many others.

Since I am just one person with one point of view, to more accurately portray what has been going on I've decided to use headlines and articles from news sites that did their best to document the events as they unfolded, to chronicle their interpretations of what happened to humanity. I've also included drawings. I don't just write children's books, I also illustrate them. I guess I have more in common with those cave artists than I'd like to admit.

The articles and illustrations will help me feel like I'm more in my element. I wish these were just drawings for children's books. Unfortunately, they are what they are: visual aids to assist in the recounting, step by step, of how things went so wrong so quickly for all of us.

From The Seattle Times, four days after the black dandelions first appeared

Botanists Baffled by Blooming of Black Dandelions

By Marcia Quinlan @MarciaQReports
April 26, 2045

What was considered an isolated event in India four days ago, has now become a global phenomenon as black dandelions are being spotted all over the world.

Researchers initially regarded last week's sighting of the first ever recorded black dandelion, a solitary flower sprouting along a frequently traveled railroad track in Delhi, as an anomaly, an unusual mutation. Now, with these strange black dandelions being spotted everywhere from Ireland to New Zealand, it is becoming clear that the mutation may not be as uncommon as was originally expected.

While many of the photos posted on social media and sent to news outlets in the days following the viral image of a boy plucking the dandelion from the Delhi train tracks were originally considered to be hoaxes, botanists worldwide have confirmed that these strange charcoal-colored flowers are indeed dandelions, and that they are nearly identical in genetic composition to the yellow weeds that terrorize lawns and fields worldwide.

The black coloring cannot be explained outside of being a mutated variant of the standard yellow weed. While perplexed over the nature and cause of this mutation, authorities maintain that there is nothing dangerous about the plant, and many have taken to collecting and even selling these black dandelions. Reminiscent of the Dutch Tulip craze in the early 1600s, some were charging exorbitant amounts for these black weeds only days ago, selling a single dandelion for as much as four hundred dollars. Now that they are sprouting up literally everywhere, people who had paid a fortune for the flowers are feeling as though they have been fleeced.

Enjoy the black dandelions while you can, no one can say for certain whether they're here to stay.

When I first saw the photo of the little boy plucking the black dandelion from the train tracks and heard about the fervor it had caused all over the internet and on the news, I didn't understand all the commotion. Mutations happen in nature all the time. Every once in a while you get a two headed cow or two headed snake, a three eyed fish or a six limbed goat. And sometimes you get a black dandelion.

It wouldn't be the first flower in history to pop up with miscolored petals. I didn't think it was a big deal. Just a little mutated, miscolored weed all the way in India. I didn't get why everyone was making such a fuss about it.

The day before the article above was printed, when I heard that there were now black dandelions sprouting up in England and on the rolling hills of Scotland, I thought it was becoming a pretty interesting phenomenon. When I saw verified photos of the little weeds growing through the cracks of the roads and sidewalks of the Las Vegas Strip, I was awestruck along with the rest of the world. It was fascinating but also a bit unnerving. When another day had passed and I heard the news of black dandelions growing on and around the pyramids of Egypt, I became concerned. And I fully understood, by that point, what all the fuss was about.

That was the same day The Seattle Times article was published. On that day, just after I'd seen the photo of the pyramids of Giza dotted all over, those small black flowers growing out from the cracks between their blocks, I looked out of the window of my den. It was early spring, and I was contemplating adding a tree or two to the front lawn. The idea of planting something, particularly trees, now after all that has happened, is funny in a twisted sort of way. But nothing was funny when I saw the first black dandelion growing out there on my lawn, standing out from among a group of the yellow variety. That was when I went from being concerned to being outright scared.

I'm not sure why I reacted the way I did, but I immediately went out, put on my sturdiest gardening gloves, grabbed a trowel and my trusty weed puller, and went to the black dandelion on my lawn. I tore it out of the grass by the root, then did the same with the yellow ones. I didn't go back into the house until my yard was entirely green. Afterward, I kept peeking out of my den window to make sure it stayed green throughout the day. I can't say why, I just had a bad feeling.

That feeling didn't get any better the following morning when I woke up. The first thing I did after getting into my chair was to go to the window. That was when my feeling went from bad to worse. The lawn that had been green less than a full day before was now spotted everywhere with black dandelions.

I spent a great deal of that day looking up news on the black dandelions, trying to understand why I was seeing so many of them in my yard. Not only were they popping up everywhere standard dandelions could be expected to grow (like on my lawn and those of my neighbors), but they were growing in places weeds didn't normally grow. I've mentioned the pyramids in Egypt; I also saw articles and images showing that the black flowers were springing up in the Sahara and Gobi Deserts. They were showing up in rainforests too, both in Brazil and Australia, growing all over the trunks and limbs of the trees like a fungus. The world was rivetted in a way it hadn't been since the COVID-19 pandemic two decades ago (around the time I lost my legs).

That had been a doozy of a time, but once it passed we all thought that sort of worldwide panic was behind us for good. This was the first time since then it felt like every eye in the world was looking at the same thing. In this case, it was black dandelions, fields of them everywhere.

The experts stayed their course, stating that the black flowers were a mutation, a freak occurrence, something to be awed by but not afraid of. Still, it was all anyone could think of and talk about, which is why the other major news of that week was so easy to overlook, to not give much thought to. The black dandelions made everyone pay very little attention to the forecasts of windstorms all over America and the rest of the world.

To be fair, they weren't described as windstorms everywhere, and the severity of those storms varied from location to location. In Daphnis and around Seattle, we received a special "Weather Advisory." High winds were expected for the end of April and the first week of May.

I wasn't too concerned about the advisory, not for myself anyway. If I had to leave the house, I would do so in my truck. High wind wouldn't be an issue. My concern when it came to the weather was how it would impact Eunice. And impact her, it did.

It turned out that it was on the first of all those windy days that the trouble would really start; April 30, four days after the first black dandelion had shown up on my lawn, a Sunday morning on which Eunice decided to go out for her usual run despite the harsh weather. I suppose that's where this story really starts.

Headlines from the last weekend of April 2045

From CBS News:

Denver Weather: High Wind Sunday Could Create Flight Delays, Property Damage, Dust Storms on the Plains

From the CBC:

Damaging Winds on the Way Sunday for Toronto as Temperatures Soar

From Global News:

Hurricane-Force Winds Blow Off Rooftops with Highest Wind Speeds on Record in England

From The Guardian:

Dozens Killed in Tropical Storm as Southern Africa Braces for More Wild Weather

Sunday, April 30, 2045

The morning of Sunday, April 30, 2045 was when our lives truly changed forever. It was four days after I had woken up to see my lawn half full of little black weeds. I hadn't bothered to pluck them out that morning. Instead, I had sprayed them with a weed killer. It wasn't the poison that was once legal decades ago. As someone who considers himself somewhat of an environmentalist, I'm a little ashamed to say that I really wished it had been the hardcore weed poison. I wanted those dandelions gone and I wasn't sure if the planet-friendly stuff would do the job. I used it nonetheless, knowing it would be a patient wait for the results.

When Sunday came and I rolled out of bed and to the window in my den to see if the weeds had begun to die, I was a bit dismayed to see that no such thing had happened. Instead, the little black flowers had turned white, as dandelions do. These had done so faster than their yellow counterparts which had sprung up at the same time.

Some people might have been happy to see those weeds sitting there like ground-bound clouds, their fluff whisking away as the wind picked up, thinking it meant they were dead. But all that meant was that their little seedlings were now being distributed around the neighborhood and onto the trails behind our grouping of houses on the cul-de-sac.

Even as most of the weeds had turned white and were being slowly blown apart by the increasing windspeeds, there were new black dandelions growing, adding to the first batch. It was disturbing.

Disturbing to me, anyway, though not everyone felt this way. My wife thought the black dandelions were beautiful, and as she walked up behind me that morning while I stared out the window, the first thing Eunice said was: "Oh no, are the black ones gone already?"

She had sounded genuinely bothered by this. Then had stated her relief when she noticed the new ones sprouting up.

We both looked out of the large bay windows, the blinds fully pulled up to take in the sight. She stood behind me, her hands on my shoulders.

Eunice was an early riser by nature. She worked a more conventional schedule than I did given her role as a financial advisor at the Bank of America. By the time I lazed my way out of bed, she was usually already dressed and ready to take on the world. This morning was no different despite it being a weekend. I didn't have to turn my head to know that she was in her running gear.

Every Sunday she ran at least five miles, rain or shine, no matter the time of year. She ran throughout the week as well, but there were few things that Eunice loved more than her Sunday jog along the trails behind our house. By that point those trails had already sprouted their own black flowers, but the black dandelions weren't the reason I didn't want Eunice heading out that day.

Even though I was frightened by them in a way I couldn't understand, I would be lying if I said I believed the black weeds were dangerous. None of this document would be believable if I was to tell you I had any idea of what they would turn out to be, and how the weather would play a role in the coming events.

"Didn't you hear about the wind warning, Eunice?" is how I responded to my wife when she told me she was leaving for her run that morning. I wasn't angry, but I wasn't exactly pleased either. "Taking one Sunday off isn't going to kill you," I added.

"A little wind isn't going to kill me either," she responded, laughing off my concern. "I've run in worse."

There wasn't much I could say to that. I'd watched her go out for runs through downpours, through the rare snowstorm. Nothing stopped her. But for some reason, some feeling I had that I couldn't explain, I wanted to stop her that Sunday. I couldn't though, and I regret that more than just about anything in my life.

She kissed me on the cheek before saying goodbye. I begrudgingly wished her a good run, letting her know I'd have breakfast ready for her when she got back. She thanked me, then left, practically running out of the house. I could hear the wind whipping around out there in the short time it had taken her to open the door and exit. It didn't make my bad feeling any better.

I'll remember that brief conversation forever. I'll always feel guilty about practically reprimanding her for sticking to her routine. When things began to go wrong with Eunice, I couldn't help but be upset with her for not listening to me that morning. Can you imagine that? I feel sick thinking it. I considered not writing that bit at all, but I want this to be an honest account of the events as they occurred, and of how I and others reacted to this unexpected dilemma.

I'm not much different than anyone else; when things don't go well, I look for someone or something to blame. When Eunice started getting sick, there was plenty of blame to go around. I blamed the wind; I definitely blamed those fucking black dandelions (excuse my language but that's part of the honesty in this); I blamed the scientists for getting it so wrong; and I blamed the newscasters for spreading that misinformation, even though I knew they were only doing their jobs. I blamed the police and the government. Worst of all, I blamed Eunice. It was only for a moment, but I did. I will never forgive myself for that. And it never left my mind the entire time she struggled for her life. Because, during that time, I couldn't help but resent her for not listening to the weather report, or to me.

I blamed a lot of things when life started to go sideways. But for having had that reaction to Eunice, all of the blame should go to me. It was irrational of me to blame her at all. It would be like being upset with a dove for flying or a dolphin for swimming, because of course she was going to go running no matter what I said, or what the weather was like. Determined doesn't begin to define her. Eunice is the most bullheaded person I've ever known.

After she left for her run, I went about my usual Sunday routine, which included watching cartoons. I think that day it was the newest addition to the Dragon Ball series. It played in the background as I got myself ready to send my latest edition of The Adventures of Freddy the Fearless Feline to my editor and closest friend (other than Eunice), a man named Derby Reynolds who I had known since my walking days when we were both English students at Washington State University.

Derby was one of the few people who hadn't been put off by my losses and my disfigurements to remain in touch with me after I went through what I went through shortly after dropping out of school. He also happens to be one of the smartest and kindest people I've ever known. He was a source of encouragement during those dark times, just by keeping in touch and asking how I was doing, and by not treating me like a circus freak after my accident.

I hadn't fully appreciated him then. However, years after, when Eunice had helped me come up with the idea for Freddy the Fearless Feline, he was the first person I reached out to for his opinion, and his editing skills. It became a partnership that proved profitable over the years. And a friendship that I thought of as priceless.

I sent him an email that morning about the new book. He replied promptly, letting me know that he wasn't feeling well and was heading to the hospital to see what the issue was. He suspected it was an allergic reaction. A skin rash and irritated eyes. Nothing too serious, but he was getting it checked out as a precaution. I wished him a speedy recovery, taking him at his word that it wasn't serious while looking forward to his feedback once he was feeling better.

It's hard to imagine now being excited about my bi-monthly story featuring a three-legged cat, but I was legitimately enthusiastic then. As though something so insignificant truly mattered. My excitement lasted until Eunice came crashing through the door. She was back far earlier than I expected, and was red-faced, rubbing her eyes, and cursing up a storm similar to the one she had run in from. She sprinted straight to the bathroom.

I'll always remember her rushing into the house. With my wife being a self-proclaimed "clean freak" (someone who complained when I didn't wipe my wheels before entering the house), I recall thinking that the situation must have been serious if she hadn't bothered to take off her shoes. Even though the bathroom was only a few feet from the entrance, this was a huge no-no for Eunice.

I asked her if she was okay from the entryway of the den, not far from the front and bathroom doors. She hadn't bothered closing the bathroom door behind her and I could hear the faucet running full blast. She said to me: "I got something in my eye while I was running. A *lot* of somethings. They weren't kidding about that storm."

I fought the urge to say "I told you so." Looking back on how things turned out, I'm extremely glad that I refrained from that small bit of arrogance. I remember that clearly. What I remember just as clearly is the relief I felt when she came out of the bathroom, still rubbing her eyes but smiling despite the fact that they were red and watery.

"You told me so, I know," she said, before rolling those reddened eyes and chuckling through her discomfort. She was beautiful even then. I recall that clearly too.

She told me she was heading to the bathroom in our bedroom to get properly cleaned up. I told her that I would be in the kitchen cooking the eggs I'd promised her. Before we parted ways, she leaned over and gave me a kiss. A kiss I'll never forget.

Now, as I sit writing this journal... this document (I'm not sure what to call it), I wish I remembered the moments before that kiss just as crisply. Not only the memories of that morning but of the mundane days we all forget; the days that blend together.

I distinctly remember how we met, all that we meant to each other, the wedding, the big decisions. I recall those very clearly. But I wish I had savored the little things: the insignificant date nights, our adventures along the boardwalk, nights out at the movies, restaurants, the ordinary events that no one really takes the time to absorb and appreciate, because no one ever thinks it'll be the last time they get to enjoy any of those things. I barely have those memories other than in a sort of vague and hazy grouping of recollections.

It's as if each thing we did regularly has been put in a different drawer of a filing cabinet – the meals out are in one drawer, movies and shows in another, vacations in a third – but no one took the time to sort these files into clear compartments within their drawers. I wish I had. But I suppose this document, this file, is the only one that really matters. Unfortunately, it is reserved for the drawer in that cabinet that is labeled "Apocalypse."

In that cabinet full of memories is a file called "How We Met." I keep referring to it in my mind as the situation continues to worsen. I look back on the day we met because it was during the worst time of my life. Or, rather, the worst until now. I look back on that memory to remind myself that, if Eunice and I were able to get through those dark times with each other, then we can get through this dark time, again, with each other.

I met her at the cemetery, which might usually be seen as a sign of ill things to come. But it hadn't been. Not until now, I suppose, if you were to look at it that way. But that's not the way I choose to see it.

We are two out of billions in this same situation, but for a long time after we met it felt like we were the only two in the world. And we got twenty-three good years from that initial encounter. For that reason, I can't look at the cemetery meeting as a bad sign, or find it portentous that it was grief that brought us together. Because it is love that has kept us together right until the end of this. Twenty-three years before this disaster, we were simply two lost people, missing part of us and wondering what we could do to feel whole again.

I was at the cemetery to visit my parents. I had visited my mother's grave a handful of times after she died, but I hadn't been there since my father had joined her. And since a wheelchair became a permanent part of my life. It was my dad's birthday, the second since he had passed, and the first time I had worked up the nerve to visit him at his final resting place.

I hadn't been able to attend my dad's funeral. I was too busy being hospitalized and recovering from having my legs amputated from the knees down. I could have watched the funeral virtually, as many people were forced to do during those early pandemic days, but even that was too much to handle. By the time I was well enough to visit his grave, the grief was still too fresh. It remained fresh even over a year after he had died. Days like his or my mom's birthday, holidays or special occasions, brought me to feeling like their deaths had just happened.

That was because I blamed myself. And still do all these years later. However, I've since learned to accept that blame and move on rather than wallow in it like I did then. It's what they would have wanted. I didn't believe that at first, but I do now. And it was Eunice who helped me see that, the way I helped her see that she wasn't responsible for the death of her son. Though if she hadn't felt such guilt over his death, we likely wouldn't have met.

I was on the cemetery road, alone, in sight of my father's grave. My mother's final resting place was in the same section but deeper in and not visible from the road. If the weather had been good, sunny all week, I might have been able to get up the slight slope that led to her grave; the earth would have been firm enough. But this was the Pacific Northwest and it had been raining for days, including that day. I knew there was no hope of reaching my mother's grave without my wheels getting stuck in the soft muck between the road and her headstone. I'm sure she would have understood why I couldn't sit directly beside her grave. She might not have understood why

I hadn't brought a Personal Support Worker with me to give me a push, or why I had shunned PSWs altogether since learning how to get around on my own.

The truth was, I hated (and still hate) feeling like I needed help. Also, whenever I couldn't do something, when something like my mother's grave was out of my reach, I felt like it was penance, and like I deserved it. In any case, I couldn't imagine my mother being particularly pleased about my visits to her grave. On the occasions I had visited her after her death, all I'd done was stand there silently, never saying anything because I didn't know what to say. I didn't even know what to think during those early days.

Guilt, even more than grief, brought me to my parents' graves on the day I met Eunice. I felt like I went there because they would have expected me to, and they might have been angry if I continued to put off visiting them. My guilt over their deaths was one of the many things I had to work through for some time.

After sitting silently near my father's flowerless headstone for several minutes, feeling like it had been pointless to go there at all, I prepared to leave. The bus that would take me home was to be at the entrance to Serenity Hill Burial Park shortly.

I was halfway from my parents' section to the entry before I was stopped by the sound of grieving. It was coming from one of the graves not far from the road. About twenty feet in from where I sat was a woman with jet black hair. She was distraught, on her knees beside a headstone.

I wouldn't have missed the bus if I had just ignored the crying woman as I had intended to. I might have been able to ignore her and move on if it was only tears; but it was wailing. Full body heaving. It was the sort of crying that, when you witness it, makes you feel like a horrible human being for even considering going on your way without offering a word of solace or a question of concern, no matter how awkward. The question of concern I asked was: "Are you okay?"

I would be lying if I said I'd been truly interested in the answer other than in a perfunctory sense, because I already knew it. It was plainly a stupid question; the woman was far from okay, she was devastated. And whoever was within a mile of us could hear it. Luckily, there wasn't anyone around other than an old woman with white hair watering a small bush growing from the middle of a grave. I momentarily made eye contact with her. The white-haired woman gave me a look that said: *Don't look at me. Help her.* Or at least that's how I interpreted it.

The question "Are you okay?" almost always demands a lie in response. It's something that is said so it can be politely replied to with a "Yes", and both the asker and answerer can go on with their day. But she didn't lie to me. Not then, and as far as I know, not ever. I think her honesty was the first thing I fell in love with, but that would be long after this initial meeting.

I sat there on the cemetery road, looking at a woman who appeared to be in her early thirties, nearly a decade older than I at the time. She was slender (when she stood up later, I would find out she

27

was tall, too), of Korean descent, and an absolute wreck.

If I had been able to, I would have approached her then and offered her physical support, something that went beyond the idiotic question I had asked. But I couldn't, so we were both there in the rain, me sitting on the road, her on the upward slope of grass mourning over whoever it was that was buried six feet below.

"No. I'm not okay," she responded. She looked directly at me as she said this. Her hair was plastered to her head, the little makeup she wore running down her face. Her eyes were red, the skin around them swollen. There was a hint of hysteria in those eyes. She looked like someone who was facing a reality they hadn't yet accepted. I was terrified she would snap, and that I had made a mistake by stopping and asking such a silly thing.

She surprised me then by smiling the saddest smile I have ever seen, and saying: "I should be okay by now. But I'm really not, and I just don't know what to do about it." Then came the bursting sob of someone who had failed tremendously to hold back a barrage of tears. It was a wonder that she had been able to get the words out at all.

As uncomfortable as I could ever remember being, I awkwardly asked her about grief groups, or therapy. She said she had tried things of that nature but nothing had stuck.

I asked her how she was trying to cope with things. She laughed through her tears this time, and said: "I drink." I smiled and said: "I do too."

Then, because it wasn't a pickup line, it wasn't a come on, it was simply one hurt and broken person reaching out to another, I had no issue saying: "Would you like to drink together? It's better than drinking alone."

It's something I would never have said to a woman I was attracted to. At least not since before my accident. And definitely not to a woman clearly in mourning, but I think I pitied her just as much as I pitied myself then, and for that reason I saw us as equals even as I sat in the wheelchair that for so long had always made me feel like less.

In any case, I expected her to say no just as I had expected her to say that she was okay and dismiss me after my first question, but she surprised me again.

She placed the flowers she had in her hands carefully and delicately near the headstone of what I would later find out was her son's grave. She then warned me that I better be ready for an earful if I really meant it about going for drinks.

We left the cemetery together. She abandoned her car in the parking lot as she walked beside me to a bar not far from Serenity Hill.

We drank that early afternoon, probably too much. Like she had promised, she gave me an earful. I was fine with that because I wasn't ready to talk yet. Though I would have plenty of time to share, as it turned out. Meeting up with each other not far from the cemetery became a weekly occurrence. However, it would be a long while before we actually entered the burial park together again. Instead, we drank nearby while talking about the people in there. We became therapists to one another.

This all took place in the spring of 2022, shortly after the COVID-19 pandemic had begun to wind down. Because of this, our talks often centered around that locked down and isolated time and how it had changed our lives. Both of us in very different ways.

"Chips on the table. If we drink, we spill," Eunice said to me one of those afternoons at the bar. She mixed and combined metaphors a lot. It was one of the things I loved about her even before I realized I loved things about her. I knew what she meant, and it was terrifying. I hadn't laid my chips on the table in a long time. And I certainly hadn't spilled my guts about what had put me in my chair, or my part in my parents' deaths to anyone I had just met. But with her it was easy because she allowed herself to be vulnerable. Her raw honesty drew the same out of me. After a while our chips were on the table, her raising the stakes and me calling each time.

When she told me that the pandemic had made her realize her marriage had been a failed one and had negatively impacted her son, I let her know that I could relate in some small way. Not to her, but to her son, even though I was much older than he was when it happened. I was a junior in college when the pandemic hit. And by the time it was in full force, I had quit school and moved back home because of the stress of it all, the inconsistency and uncertainty that had become pandemic life. Because of that, I had to listen to every minute of my parents fighting over their issues.

When selecting colleges, I had picked Washington State University because of its location relative to where my family and I lived. My campus in Pullman was nearly a six-hour drive from our home in Daphnis. Close enough to come back to visit when I wanted to, but far enough to avoid the same tension that I had grown up around for long stretches of time.

I stayed in a rental house I shared with a few other students near campus throughout the summer, essentially making it my home. Coming back to see my parents on holidays as a visitor had been good for all of us. Everyone is on their best behavior for a visitor, even such a familiar one. I had fooled myself into believing that their best behavior was their new normal behavior. I had convinced myself that things had improved between them with me gone.

Moving back in after two years away, I was disappointed to find out that my mother had been lying when she'd said my father had been slowing down on the drinking and had become calmer in general after I had moved out. When I moved back home, I found out quickly that he was still drinking, and he was harder to deal with than ever.

Eunice raised the stakes when she told me that her husband had drunk heavily as well. The longer the lockdown went on, the worse it got. One night, after an argument she couldn't recall the details of, he hit her. It wasn't the first time in their relationship that he'd struck her, but it was the first time in a long time. He apologized, of course, tearfully. And did so each time he hit her after that.

In response to this truth, I offered the fact that I had stolen my dad's car one night when my parents had had a particularly loud fight. I wasn't sure why I'd taken it. Maybe I'd thought that if they noticed me and the car gone, in addition to everything that was going on in the world, they might put what was important in perspective. Or maybe I'd just needed to leave and get far away. Either way, they hadn't noticed that I'd stolen the car, or even that I was gone.

Eunice let me know that she would have still been with her ex being slapped about the face if not for the fact that her husband had eventually started hitting their child. That was when she considered making a middle of the night drive, as I had. Except she had wanted to take her son as well. And never return. Her biggest mistake, she told me while taking generous sips of the house special on tap, was that she'd only considered making that drive, and hadn't done it. Instead, she'd threatened her husband, telling him that she would leave him and take their boy if he laid his hands on either one of them again.

I told her that I had gone to an illegal house party the night I had stolen the car. About two dozen people from my high school and a handful of others I didn't know had been in attendance. It was one of many pandemic parties that were all the rage during those lockdown days.

She let me know that her husband had offered an apology again, which she had accepted again. When she woke up the next morning, her husband was gone.

I told her that I drove home drunk the night of that pandemic party. I told her that it was the last time I had danced. But that I somehow made it home safely. And that my getting home safely was the last blessing

I would have (I said this not realizing what a blessing getting to know her was, not at that point).

She told me that, after noticing her husband gone, she had found her son murdered in his bed, his face pale, his little lips blue beneath his pillow. It was her husband's idea of ultimate control. If the boy wasn't alive, how could she take him?

I informed her that I had contracted COVID-19 at the pandemic party, and gave it to both of my parents. Three weeks later, it killed my mother. My father recovered from the illness but never from losing my mom. Five months after her death, the grief killed him. The grief received an assist from many, many pills, and copious amounts of booze.

She let me know that her husband had been caught less than a day after he'd fled from their home. The police had found him asleep in a stolen car parked behind a strip mall not far from the border. He had planned to head for Canada after killing their son but hadn't considered that the border was closed at that time due to the pandemic.

I told her that, after I had discovered my father's corpse (he had died sitting in his favorite spot in front of the television in the living room with a glass of rum in front of him), I had stolen his car again. Not knowing what else to do, I drove. And while this time it had been the middle of the day and I hadn't had a drop of alcohol in me, my head had been clouded, my eyes blurred. I let her know that I had run a red light, resulting in a van T-boning my father's Volkswagen Jetta.

Thankfully, the other driver only suffered minor injuries. I, however, wound up in a wheelchair minus both legs from the knees down.

She told me that she had slept on her four-year-old son's uncovered and urine-stained mattress for over a year before her sister forced her to get rid of it and the house her family had lived in.

We both cried, we both drank, and we both left all our chips on the table. For weeks we would meet to rehash these events, cry, and eventually, every once in a while, find something we could laugh about.

It took me too long to ask her out officially, and I'd been terrified when I finally worked up the nerve to say the words: "Maybe we can go somewhere else next week? You know, like on an actual date."

She'd looked horrified. I'll never forget how foolish I felt when I saw how she looked at me. How she wrinkled her face in an expression of almost comical disbelief (comical if it hadn't made me shrink in my chair from embarrassment). I almost told her to forget it, to just never mind what I had said. But she got her words out before I did mine, and called my raising of the stakes once again when she said: "I'm a bit disappointed... and embarrassed. I thought dating was what we've been doing this entire time."

That was how we met, and how I asked her out two months after she had already known we were dating and (according to her) that we would be together forever. I had to write that out because I never have. I've never really detailed the story of how two broken people got together and made it work. The story of how we fixed each other. It's a story that is the world to me now as I look back at things. A world that will never be the same again.

That's why I relish the memory of our first date (that I realized we were on) just as much as I do the memory of the kiss we shared when she came back home on that Sunday morning, rubbing her eyes after a run through the windstorm. After each of these events the world changed in a way that could never be revoked. Except this time around it was the entire world, not just mine. It was everybody's existence that would never be the same.

From MLB.com on April 30, 2045

Sunday Night Baseball game between Yankees and Red Sox postponed due to high winds

Game will be rescheduled as part of a double header when the Yankees return to Boston in July

By Morgan Martin @MMartinMLB
4:02 PM PST

The Red Sox announced the postponement less than two hours before the first scheduled pitch at Fenway Park. Many of the ballpark's employees had already arrived for work and fans who had braved the conditions were milling around outside the gates when the game was postponed.

The sun was out, but there was rain in the forecast and winds were gusting at the time of the postponement.

The Yankees and Red Sox played in steady wind and blowing rain on Saturday afternoon, conditions that several players on both teams said were among the worst they had ever played in. The second game of the three-game series was officially stopped in the bottom of the seventh with Boston leading 11-2.

It didn't seem like the world was set to change in a way that couldn't be remedied that Sunday after Eunice had returned home from her short run. While she stayed in the bedroom for most of the rest of the day after complaining about the irritation in her eyes, I spent much of the afternoon doing what I always did on Sunday afternoons: streaming the Seattle Mariners game.

It was a bittersweet season. The Mariners were finally expected to make a push for the World Series; that was the sweet part. The bitter part was that it was also the last season to be played at Safeco Field (it was under sponsorship by some other company by then, but I grew up when it was Safeco and it'll always be that to me).

They would have to abandon the stadium as the city prepared for what the government was calling a "retraction" but was really the beginning of the process of abandoning the city altogether. Water levels were rising, seaside houses were already flooded, and most of the citizens of Seattle would have to be relocated by 2050. The stadium and much of the city surrounding it was expected to be flooded and deemed uninhabitable by then. It was essentially the same in New York City, Miami, and many other coastal cities around the world.

We had been hearing about climate change for decades, hearing the politicians debate its existence. Their opinions on the matter mostly dependent on how the idea of addressing global warming helped their chances at re-election, or how attempting to change things would impact whatever industry they had an interest in.

I remember those debates, the news stories we ignored, the articles a lot of us scrolled past on social media. It all just seemed like theater in those days. Then, in 2040, we got the alert that much of Seattle would have to be evacuated by the end of the decade. All at once it was interactive, participatory theater, and we were right there with the actors, no longer able to easily separate ourselves from the show.

People of all sorts suddenly cared more when they were at risk of being homeless. We in Daphnis were fortunate to be further inland in Washington. We didn't have to worry about moving, but we did have to worry about the rapid development of the area. Condos were sprouting up everywhere; our small city was becoming larger and louder. The fresh air we once relished was already a thing of the past, much like most of Seattle would soon be. What no one wanted to talk about was how long it would be before Daphnis was next. That wouldn't just be theater, it would be a circus.

The Mariners won, that's what I remember about one of the last baseball games that might ever be played (at least for a very long time to come). The Mariners walked it off: a double down the right field line by our star first baseman to win it in the bottom of the tenth. It was a thrilling game. I was planning on watching the Sunday Night Baseball game between the Yankees and Red Sox, but it was called off due to excessive wind. The windstorm wasn't only wreaking havoc here on the west coast, it was countrywide.

With the Sunday Night Baseball game cancelled, I opted to stream the live local evening news where the topics of the night, aside from a few crimes and an update on the pollution index (which by then was given as regularly as the temperature), were the windstorms and the black dandelions.

Watching the news was as fascinating as it was disturbing. Even then I had no idea of the trouble we were all in, mainly because the news reporters were doing a good job of downplaying what was going on. That or they were doing a great job of spreading their blissful ignorance.

There were sports updates, a brief update about the upcoming evacuation process of Seattle. There was mention of pink eye going around King County along with a warning from the broadcasters to keep kids from playing too close together, advising them to wash their hands and not to rub their eyes.

There was the usual joking and banter between reporter and meteorologist as they talked about the strange phenomenon of the dandelions and the windstorms. And how the wind was likely to wreak havoc on people's allergies as dust and pollen, spores and seeds from the dandelions whipped through the air. The good news was that the winds would be calming down by the end of the workweek, just in time for us to enjoy a rainy weekend. They had chuckled at that.

The newscast went to their go-to horticulturalist, a short, thin fellow nicknamed Green Thumb Tom. He advised that, unlike the wind, the dandelions might be around to stay all summer, but they could be killed just like standard dandelions could. I thought of the weedkiller I had sprayed all over them a few days prior and wondered if that was true.

"With the wind blowing the dandelion seeds around like crazy, these weed killer sprays and weed removal tools are a must to have in your toolshed or garage this gardening season," Green Thumb Tom had said, then went on to list a number of recommended products. I was annoyed to find out that the product I had used was not on his list.

The potential hassle of the dandelions interested me far more than the wind patterns across the country. High winds have become far more common now than when I was a kid. Something to do with global warming and rising temperatures worldwide. High water and high wind. While the former was thought to be a fundamental disaster, particularly in the coastal states where towns were being evacuated, the wind was thought to be a blessing in disguise. It wasn't normally as severe as it would be over the days following Eunice's ill-fated run, but the increase in wind had done wonders for the push toward renewable energy.

Wind turbines were popping up everywhere in the world. Most thought this was too little too late, particularly because of the amount of pollution many countries had pumped into the air and oceans since the industrial age. Sadly, despite everything that had been going on, some countries still refused to take significant measures to reduce their output of waste and greenhouse gases.

I was reminded during this newscast that there was to be a meeting of world leaders in the upcoming weeks to decide on new wording for yet another Environmental Accord. It was meant to be held in Tokyo. Japan, like many other nations, was having monumental issues regarding what to do with their nuclear waste. The newscast went into this in greater detail, but by that point I had tuned out. I suppose that was part of the problem.

It was late into the evening by then. Eunice hadn't made much noise from the bedroom since retiring there before noon. She hadn't even come out to have lunch or dinner. I went to check in on her again. Earlier, she had complained that the irritation in her eyes was bringing on an intense headache.

When I got to the bedroom it was completely dark. I could hear what sounded like a movie podcast playing from Eunice's phone on the nightstand beside our bed. She didn't seem to be listening to it. She was asleep, and it didn't appear to be a peaceful sleep. She was muttering something I couldn't hear, and her arm was draped over her eyes.

The most concerning thing was the smell in the room. It smelled like a mixture of sweat and freshly cut grass. At first, I thought it was coming in from outside, but the windows were closed. I remember hoping she wasn't coming down with something, a cold or the flu, something from running outdoors while in a sweat so often. I had no clue it would turn out to be what it would turn out to be.

I left her in the bed and went back to the den, which was also my library, television room, and office. I stayed there the rest of the night working on the artwork for Freddy the Fearless Feline's next adventure. I let the news play in the background for a bit before streaming some lighthearted sitcoms from my teens and settling in on the couch with my third beer of the night and a bowl full of pretzels. I planned to camp out there, so as not to disturb Eunice. I still wonder if deciding to sleep on the couch that night might have saved me from a great deal of misery.

From a conspiracy site called Read Between the Lies

THE GOVERNMENT IS LYING: BLACK DANDELIONS A BIOENGINEERING EXPERIMENT GONE WRONG

By Robert Brandini @Readbetweenthelies
May 1, 2045

Don't believe them. Don't believe the people on the mainstream newsfeeds and networks. They are lying to you. And they are lying to you on behalf of the government. These black dandelions aren't just some mutation or abnormality. They are a sign of a bioengineering experiment gone wrong.

This is simply a failed attempt at fixing what they call global warming (another problem caused by their experimentation on the world and weather).

My sources tell me that the government was working on a new prolific vegetable that would sprout as quickly as dandelions, wouldn't require much tending to, and would solve a lot of our problems. The real problem is that they messed up. Now we have these poisonous plants popping up everywhere, and there's no telling what they're going to do to us.

As always, stay vigilant, stay safe, stay smart. And Read Between the Lies.

Monday, May 1, 2045

I don't know why I go to conspiracy websites as much as I do. I'm not a conspiracy guy per se, but I don't like to dismiss them outright either. I mean, there are the really crazy ones that are laughable, but sometimes there's a bit of truth to some conspiracies. At the very least, they're entertaining; it's both funny and scary to see the wild things people come up with.

On Monday morning, the day after Eunice's run, it was the scary side of the conspiracies I had been reading lately that I thought of when I saw my wife.

Eunice was worse than she had been the day before. She had stumbled into the den before shaking me awake. She still had a slight headache, but the concerning thing was that she said she was having trouble seeing. She said it felt like she had a film over her eyes. I think her exact words were: "Its like someone put a pair of pantyhose over my head. I can see, but it's a blur."

We went to an optometrist instead of to a doctor, which is almost laughable when I look at how bad it has gotten since. I suggested the emergency room, but Eunice wouldn't hear of it. She hated hospitals in general, and particularly loathed the emergency room. She avoided doctors as though they were responsible for the illnesses they diagnosed. She could be stubborn, to put it mildly. The fact that she had suggested going to the optometrist at all let me know how serious it was.

Our optometrist's office was over an hour away, practically in Seattle, and further than I liked to drive, but Eunice happened to know someone who worked there. Her friendship with Ruth, the receptionist, was the only reason we went to that particular eye doctor, and was the reason we could be squeezed into the schedule to see her that same morning.

Before I drove us to the doctor, I put on a pair of glasses. They were non-prescription blue light glasses I used when working on my computer for extended periods of time. I didn't need them for driving but thought it would be best to use them as a bit of protection from everything that was flying around outside. It was still powerfully windy, and the dandelion fluff was everywhere. It looked like light snow on a gloomy, windy, winter day. There was an occasion or two during the drive that I thought I would have to use the windshield wipers. Luckily it didn't come to that.

After examining Eunice, Dr. Gillian Singh said that it seemed to be an eye infection. Conjunctivitis was the word she used before dumbing it down and referring to it as pink eye for us layfolk. I looked at my wife as she squinted at me. She looked as though she had been blasted with bear mace. Her eyes were far beyond pink. But the doctor guaranteed us that that was all it was. She told us in a voice that made me feel reassured that, with the wind blowing around as it was, and with people getting things into their eyes and trying to rub those things out, a few people had caught the eye infection one way or another. They were likely going to spread it if they weren't careful like we were being. I remembered hearing mention of a breakout of pink eye on the news the night before, so her analysis made sense to me.

She recommended an antibiotic eyedrop and said to come back in a few days if things didn't start to improve. There were oral medications that could be prescribed if it persisted.

She warned us that it was contagious. That warning was likely what spared me the worst of it. The eye doctor was dead wrong about everything else, but on that count, she was spot on, and I'm glad we took her advice so seriously.

We were in and out quickly, Dr. Singh seeming more rushed that morning than during any other visit I could recall. According to Ruth at reception, a lot of people were trying to book emergency appointments that day. As we left and as Eunice continued to struggle not to rub her eyes, I remember thinking that the doctor must have downplayed how badly the spread of the conjunctivitis already was.

I recall leaving the optometrist's office very clearly because it was the last time I was truly hopeful about the situation. It was the last time things felt normal: the two of us leaving an appointment, on our way to pick up Eunice's prescription and get past what should have been an insignificant case of pink eye. We even talked about the vacation days Eunice had remaining for the year, and what we would do with her time off. We agreed it would have to be spent at least partially in Seattle. We wanted to take advantage of the city while it was still above water.

We chatted about the influx of people who would be moving from Seattle to Daphnis in the upcoming years and how that might change things for our city. I updated her on the Mariner's game from the day before. It was a normal drive home. And it remained a mostly normal day.

The next time we left our house we would be stepping into an entirely different world.

Because of the doctor's instructions about pink eye being contagious, Eunice and I stayed separate for the entire day and through the night. She stayed in the bedroom while I remained in the den, which I didn't mind. I had always found the couch in there more comfortable than our bed.

I watched TV and she listened to her podcasts while laying in bed. With her eyes as blurry as they were, she couldn't do much else. We yelled back and forth when something of interest or of note came up. I brought her food, which she didn't have much of an appetite for. I administered her eyedrops every few hours as per the instructions of the pharmacist (careful to wear a pair of swimming goggles to prevent myself from catching what she had).

As I helped her with her eyedrops, I noticed a light green discharge seeping slowly out from beneath her eyelids. It concerned me, but I had done a quick search on the web after we had returned home from seeing Dr. Singh, and learned that conjunctivitis could cause that sort of symptom if it was severe enough. I thought nothing more of it, wiping the discharge away, putting in her eyedrops and washing my hands thoroughly when I was done with the process. She said she felt fine other than the blurry eyes and headache, and I believed her. It was an odd night, but it wasn't a bad one.

Eventually, we wished each other good night from the distance between our bedroom and my temporary quarters in the den. I told her to call out if she needed anything. That was around 10:00 PM. Five hours later, she took me up on that offer.

Tuesday, May 2, 2045

"Honey? Alex?" The sound of Eunice's voice woke me up. Thankfully (during times like this, at least), I'm an extremely light sleeper. There was panic in her voice, and I think if I had taken any longer to respond to her, she might have begun to scream.

"Everything okay, Eunice?" I called back into the darkness. Sitting upright, I commanded the house to turn the lights on before lifting myself into my wheelchair. The brightness blurred my sight and nearly made me rub my eyes. I stopped myself from doing so when I thought of the condition my wife was in.

When Eunice responded to my question, I no longer had the urge to rub my eyes, everything became clear to me. She said: "I'm not sure... I... My eyes, they've gotten worse."

I rolled over to our bedroom as quickly as I could. I was going to go straight to the bed, but she called out again just as I entered the room. She warned me to stay back, and I saw that she was raising a somewhat limp hand toward me like a traffic cop calling for cars to come to a stop. She said: "Careful, Alex. I'm feeling a bit feverish too."

She looked feverish. She didn't look good in general. I rolled closer to her, but not too close. "You okay, honey?" I said.

It was one of those silly questions I sometimes asked. She was patient with me as always, saying: "Not so much. I feel like I'm coming down with something other than the pink eye. But even that's getting worse. I can barely see anything."

She told me that she could still see shapes and a bit of light but not much else. I looked at her eyes, and it was a wonder she could see anything at all. The green discharge that I had wiped away the night before had come back with a vengeance. It looked like a thin layer of moss had begun to grow from out of her eyes, coating her eyelashes and threatening to cover her eyelids entirely. The optometrist had said that it might get worse before it got better, but she hadn't mentioned anything like this. Nor had I seen anything like this while researching conjunctivitis online.

Looking at her there, her eyes all gummed up and her skin pale and covered with a thin layer of sweat, I made the decision for both of us. We had to head to the hospital.

I only noticed the smell again when we began discussing how we would navigate to the car without her being able to see. I noticed that she smelled like dirt. I don't mean that disrespectfully or crudely, I mean she literally smelled like dirt. Like grass and soil after a hard rain. I attributed it to her sweat-dampened clothes. Fever sweat nearly always smelled rank.

Ignoring the smell, I left the room to grab my goggles and a medical mask. I got a mask for her as well. Masks are a staple in a lot of households these days. Not only thanks to lingering paranoia from the pandemic of the early 20s but also because of the pollution. Smog alerts were a regular occurrence all over the country. It wasn't the smog I was concerned about now, however; I was hoping to everything holy that I wouldn't catch what she had.

Returning to the room, I got her purse, my wallet, and keys from the dresser. I put them all in my lap and reversed my way to the bed.

When I had positioned my chair within arm's reach of her, I let her know I was there beside the bed. She followed my voice until she stood behind me with her hands on the handles of my chair. I wheeled forward and she walked behind me, holding on to my handles all the while. We stayed that way, making it slowly through the house and to my pickup truck.

Once we got outside, I helped her into the truck before going around to the driver's side of the vehicle. I was relieved to find that the wind had died down since the previous day. A small mercy given the circumstances.

The process of getting into the truck from my wheelchair had never felt so arduous and time consuming. I lifted myself out of my chair and into the swivel car seat, then pressed the button that would allow a device in the bed of the truck (what I called the Hook and Hoist) to lift my wheelchair from the driveway and into the bed of the truck. Usually, the process didn't bother me at all, but after looking at the moss-like green discharge growing out of Eunice's eyes from a close distance, I wanted to be at the hospital immediately. Teleporting wouldn't have been fast enough.

It wasn't only the discharge I was concerned about. Something else that troubled me was that Eunice had developed a rash on her face and on the back of her hands that hadn't been there before; her skin had been red after she had come back from her run, but I had assumed that was due to the wind.

Looking at my wife and wondering what could have gotten into her system terrified me. It nearly sent me into a panic. I wanted to take several deep breaths to steady myself, but I didn't want to risk pulling in whatever she might be stricken with. I rolled down the window, took a mask-filtered breath of the outdoor air, and drove.

It was nearly four in the morning by the time I left our driveway. If I was going to speed, now was the time to do it. There wasn't a soul in sight. I planned to crank the hand control and pick up the pace once we got off the residential streets, but I never got the chance to truly speed that early morning because we didn't make it to the hospital. We didn't even make it out of the neighborhood.

My usual route to the freeway was down Riverside Avenue to Centennial Road. When we got to the intersection of Riverside and Centennial, I slowed down. I couldn't believe what I was looking at. I swore loudly. I can't remember which curse words exactly, but there were a lot of them. The kind you say when you are seeing something you don't believe and, more importantly, that you don't want to see. A reaction to something that is impeding you from heading somewhere crucial.

"What is it?" Eunice asked me. She sounded too tired for my liking. I had to remind myself that it was before dawn, and that she hadn't slept soundly to put my mind at ease over just how tired she sounded. I would have told her why I was swearing, except the reason that I was swearing beat me to it. From one of the several vehicles blocking the intersection ahead of us came a booming announcement:

"PLEASE RETURN TO YOUR HOME. THERE IS A QUARANTINE IN EFFECT AS OF MIDNIGHT. PLEASE RETURN TO YOUR HOME IMMEDIATELY AND VISIT THE CITY'S WEBSITE FOR MORE INFORMATION."

I initially thought it was a recording. The voice was cold and unemotional. It repeated the message another time and I could hear it sounded slightly different than the first. There was someone watching us from inside one of those vehicles ahead of us, though I couldn't tell which vehicle exactly.

Directly at the end of Riverside, blocking our way to Centennial, were what appeared to be two SWAT vehicles; two large black vehicles that looked like a cross between a delivery truck and an army tank. Along with these, a black SUV was parked on the eastern shoulder of the road to my right. Further behind these was a large red truck sitting diagonally in the intersection, making it impossible for traffic to pass through from any direction. I thought it was a fire engine until I looked at it closely and saw the words on the side of it:

STATE OF WASHINGTON
EMERGENCY RESPONSE

Beneath those words was written:

HAZARDOUS MATERIALS DECONTAMINATION UNIT

I didn't reverse. My wife and I sat there quietly. I badly wanted to hold her hand, but I knew I shouldn't touch her. There was a quarantine apparently, and I felt like it was because of whatever she was ill with. I quickly crossed conjunctivitis off my list of possibilities for that illness, understanding at that point that our eye doctor had been wrong.

I thought about the announcement that had come from the direction of the roadblock: a quarantine as of midnight. I wondered why I hadn't heard anything about it. Then I remembered that I had turned off my phone and put it away before going to sleep. That was well before midnight when the alert might have been sent out. If there had been an emergency alert at all, I had slept right through it. Eunice likely had done the same. Neither of us had thought of our mobile devices while scrambling to get to the hospital.

I was too frustrated and desperate to listen to the instructions that had boomed in our direction from the vehicles in our path. I wanted answers, Eunice needed help. I inched forward again.

"DO NOT ADVANCE ANY FURTHER! PLEASE TURN YOUR VEHICLE AROUND AND HEAD BACK HOME. THERE IS A QUARANTINE IN EFFECT!"

For some reason I chose to ignore this warning again. Eunice asked me several times what was going on, but I ignored her as well. I didn't have the answers, and I was aiming to get them. I wanted an explanation and not just the insistence of this cold voice that I ought to turn around and go back to where I came from. My goal was to try to get close enough to be heard by whoever was on the loudspeaker in whichever truck it was blasting from, but I didn't get the chance.

As I proceeded forward, the back door of one of the vehicles blocking the intersection flew open. From inside of it jumped two people dressed in a peculiar fashion. They reminded me of two things at the same time. They reminded me of astronauts wearing sleeker, more streamlined suits than the norm, and they also reminded me of soldiers, because, along with the full body HAZMAT suits they wore, these two people were carrying assault weapons. And those weapons were pointed directly at us.

I stopped the truck. This time I reversed even before the cold voice boomed over the loudspeaker again, once more reminding us that we ought to go home and get quarantined. I watched the two soldiers intently as I tried to manipulate my car through the most awkward of three-point turns, not taking my eyes off their weapons. I prayed quietly that they wouldn't decide to shoot into the vehicle as I drove.

"What was that?" Eunice whispered once my truck had picked up a steady pace driving away from the roadblock. I let her know what I had seen once the soldiers and their vehicles were far in the rear-view. I kept sneaking glances at the road behind me, then ahead of me, and also at Eunice. I wanted to see how all of it was registering with her.

Even though she was still sweaty, her face was calm. I was hoping that the realization of what was going on wouldn't destroy that calm. "It's me, isn't it?"

she said. "What I have. That's what this quarantine is all about. It's not just pink eye."

"I don't know," I said to her even though I was nearly certain she was right. A part of me wanted to think it might be something else happening to someone else. Not my Eunice, my entire world. I let her know I was still planning to get her to a hospital. I asked: "How are you feeling?"

"A bit better now that I got some air," she responded. Her window was partially rolled down, as was mine. I didn't want to tell her that I was grateful for the windows being rolled down because it would mean we wouldn't be recycling stale air in the closed cabin together while whatever virus or bacteria that was attacking her body was sharing the air with us.

"Maybe we should just head home. If there's a roadblock here, there's bound to be others between here and the hospital," she said reasonably. But I wasn't in a reasonable state of mind. And I had never much liked being told what to do.

It wasn't so much what Eunice was telling me to do that bothered me, it was the disembodied voice from the vehicle at the intersection commanding me to go home that I wanted to defy. Which is why, instead of turning left back in the direction of our home when I got to the top of the street, I turned right and headed west toward the hospital. Reassuring my wife that I would get her help, I took a few lefts and rights until I got to the next major intersection that would take us to Daphnis General Hospital.

"Fuck." There wasn't anything else to say when I saw what I saw there. It was the exact same setup. A large vehicle that looked like a firetruck stretched diagonally across the intersection. There were more black trucks, and another black SUV.

"What is it?" Eunice asked, her voice sounding distressed. Once again, before I could answer, someone else answered for me. Another cold voice coming from one of those trucks. It was a female's this time. Other than that difference, it may as well have been a recording of the previous warning: "PLEASE RETURN TO YOUR HOME. THERE IS A QUARANTINE IN EFFECT AS OF MIDNIGHT. PLEASE RETURN TO YOUR HOME IMMEDIATELY AND VISIT THE CITY'S WEBSITE FOR MORE INFORMATION."

This time I didn't bother approaching the blockade. I made a much steadier three-point turn than the last attempt and headed not for home but for the next possible exit out of this grid of side streets, toward the main road and to the hospital. Along the way I saw the occasional motorist here and there, but the streets were mostly empty. I couldn't help but wonder what the roads would be like in a few hours when people headed out for work or to see loved ones, only to find that we were in some sort of extreme lockdown. I wondered how many people in the houses we drove past were in the same condition as my wife. Then I tried to fool myself into thinking that it must all be due to something else. That the quarantine must have been for some other issue, and that her situation was an isolated incident. It was an idiotic notion.

We reached a third intersection that would lead us to a main road and toward Daphnis General Hospital. This time I didn't bother to swear, and Eunice didn't bother to ask. But the voice answered nonetheless:

"PLEASE RETURN TO YOUR HOME. THERE IS A QUARANTINE IN EFFECT…"

I U-turned. I went to find another route, but I had pushed my luck one time too many. I wound up being followed out of the intersection.

Before I could let out another string of expletives, I heard the brief hoot of a siren, and flashing blue and red lights spilled into the cabin of my truck. I pulled over. Eunice groaned before saying: "We should have just gone home. I don't feel as bad as I did before. What's going on?"

I looked over at her. Even in the dark of the early morning I could see the thick mossy growth from both of her eyes. She may not have felt so bad, but she looked terrible. "It's a chaser," I told her. I wanted to sound calm, but I was stressed and scared.

The police had sent what they called a deployment drone after us. It was a piece of technology that had only been introduced and integrated starting late last decade. The deployment drones, which most people referred to as chasers, were the response to the cries for police reform in the 2020s. After the murder of George Floyd and the protests that followed, changes had to be made. It took a while, but this new technological aspect of policing was the biggest and most dramatic of those changes.

As a way of cutting down on high-speed chases, police brutality, and false reports, each police vehicle in most major cities was equipped with a deployment drone. The drones were operated remotely by specially trained police officers, who did so from the comfort of their assigned stations.

When a person was pulled over, a drone was deployed to record the incident from overhead. If they ran, the drone would track them. Depending on the level of risk they posed, the drone might simply follow until the person fleeing decided to turn themselves in, or the drone could subdue the fleer using nonlethal force before the arrival of human backup. It turned out that most criminals chose to submit when being chased by a flying orb controlled by law enforcement.

As a Black man in America, I had been glad to hear about these advancements in police procedures when they were implemented. But at that moment I couldn't help but feel unnerved by the drone. Chasers were something most people only heard about or saw in videos online. They weren't something you ever wanted to encounter. And here was one hovering behind me.

For the fourth time that night, a voice blared out at me. Though this time the message was different: "ALEXANDER LANGSTON, YOU HAVE BEEN ASKED SEVERAL TIMES TO RETURN TO YOUR HOME. PLEASE DO AS INSTRUCTED OR RISK BEING APPREHENDED."

I wasn't surprised to hear that it knew my name. They had likely used a facial recognition scanner at the checkpoint this drone had come from. That, combined with a quick scan of my license plate, and I had officially been identified and warned by the officer operating the drone remotely and behaving as its voice. Not knowing what else to do, I made another U-turn and headed for home. The chaser drone followed behind us the entire while.

When we arrived at the house, as soon as we had exited the truck, I apologized to Eunice for letting her down. For some reason, I felt that re-entering the house would be the ultimate sign of failure, and found I needed to apologize for that failure before it happened. I'd vowed to get my wife to the hospital, and I hadn't done so. It had been decades since I'd felt so low.

She told me I hadn't let her down at all as she stood and I sat on the driveway surrounded by the windy early morning gloom. Then she put her hands on my handles and followed as I led her to the door.

I turned to see that the drone was still hovering behind us at the foot of the driveway. It was watching us to make sure we were committed to returning home. It was no longer flashing its police lights, but it still emitted a menacing red glow from what I thought of as its visor.

The chaser looked like a floating motorcycle helmet, and I knew that, behind the screen visible to me, I was being watched by whoever was monitoring it from a nearby police station. What were they thinking as they saw my wife in the condition she was in? Would I ever be able to go and get help? Would they let me? Those were the questions on my mind as I glanced back.

Then something unexpected happened. Something struck the drone. I had to do a doubletake as I saw the drone reel and then wheel its visor in the direction the object which had struck it had come from.

"Get the fuck out of here you metal monitoring piece of shit!"

Eunice and I both stalled at the sound of the commotion. I looked to my left and saw Josh, the young adult son of my neighbors who spent as much time vacationing without their kid as they did at home with him. They were currently on such a vacation. Their habitual absences often led to parties and the occasional noise complaint (usually from our other neighbor, Ben).

It looked like Josh had been hosting a small gathering when the lockdown was announced. He and two others were on his porch. Josh was shirtless, and I could see that he had something balled in his left hand. More rocks, I presumed, like the one that had hit the drone already, likely scooped up from his front garden, which was full of small decorative stones.

Making his way from the porch along the driveway toward the drone, Josh hurled another rock through the air. The drone evaded the projectile and hovered toward the house at the bottom of the cul-de-sac where the three kids barely out of their teens stood. Two of them ran back inside, but Josh stood defiantly on his driveway. The chaser seemed to carefully regard him before it said: "RETURN TO YOUR RESIDENCE. THERE IS A QUARANTINE IN EFFECT UNTIL FURTHER NOTICE. CHECK THE CITY WEBSITE FOR MORE DETAILS."

In response to this announcement, Josh grabbed his crotch with his right hand and thrust his groin in the direction of the chaser. "Quarantine THIS!" he called out. But despite his bravado, he dropped the remaining stones from his hand and backed his way toward his house.

The drone hovered for a moment longer, then turned back toward Eunice and me. I thought it would say something, that it might give me a warning similar to that it had given to Josh, but it didn't. It flew off into the sky.

When the chaser was out of sight, I looked over at Josh. I acknowledged him by way of a nod. He gave me a part-wave, part-salute of a gesture before returning to his house.

I rolled into my home while guiding my wife behind me, both of us quiet from the shock of what had happened in our city, literally overnight.

An article from the day of the lockdown, courtesy of The Daphnis Daily Herald

Extreme Lockdown Considered A 'Preventative Measure' As Unknown Contagion Spreads Across Country

By Angela Davidson @AngieDavidson
May 2, 2045

The city of Daphnis is one of many currently subject to an emergency lockdown. This lockdown is being called a preventative quarantine as a highly contagious unknown illness that targets the eyes is spreading throughout the country, and reportedly the world. As of this morning, all residents of the state of Washington are required to stay in their homes until more is known about this emerging illness, and the situation is deemed safe.

Medical authorities originally believed this to be an aggressive form of conjunctivitis, commonly known as pink eye, but have since said this is something they have not seen before. With no definitive answers, isolation seems to be the safest option at this time.

For further information, as well as details on how to obtain essential items such as groceries and medication, log on to www.daphnis.gov.

I expected chaos the rest of that morning and day.
Because of the roadblocks, I expected to hear honking
horns, angry shouts, warnings from chaser drones for
people to return home and stay there. I didn't hear
any of that, much to my surprise. Apparently, people
had taken heed of the alerts that Eunice and I had
missed and had hunkered down in their homes. The
streets were quiet because everyone was inside, glued
to their TVs or laptops or phones. I happened to be
checking in on all three.

Eunice had gone back to bed once we got home.
She complained that she felt weak, and quickly fell
asleep. I checked in on her periodically as I tried to
stay updated on what was going on using all the
forms of technology available to me. On the television,
I had a live stream of the local news. This time the
tone was much different than it had been on Sunday.
There was no more jovial banter, no talk about sports,
gardening, or environmental initiatives. There wasn't
even mention of the weather or the black dandelions.
The topic of the day was the illness that was going
around. One that had turned out not to be
conjunctivitis but a new contagion that doctors and
scientists were still trying to figure out. They listed off
the symptoms, and I remember each of them because
my wife had nearly every single one:

Red and runny eyes, including a discharge not
dissimilar to mucus; a headache ranging from slight
to severe; a fever/elevated temperature; sweating;
and emitting an odor reminiscent of freshly cut grass.
The only symptom she was lacking was a cough.

I was on high alert for that last symptom. While I
was mostly listening to the news as I scrolled on my

laptop and messaged people on my phone, I was also listening for the sound of her coughing. I hoped that, if she didn't develop the cough, she might not have had whatever was spreading. It was a foolish thought, but it was the only hope I really had to hold on to because things seemed so grim.

The newscasters on the television sounded like they were reporting on a bombing. The words "quarantine," "preventative," and "lockdown" were said repeatedly. Comparisons were made to the last time around, during the coronavirus pandemic.

I listened to a newscaster say: "The slow and unprepared response to the pandemic two decades ago from nations around the world has made it so measures that may seem extreme are being taken now. Authorities are making it clear that a pandemic has *not* officially been declared. The lockdown is a preventative measure. Thanks to legislation passed after COVID-19, there is now a Pandemic Prevention Response Plan, which unfortunately includes a countrywide lockdown. Fortunately, thanks to the PPRP, those who have to miss work will be taken care of..."

It was then that I heard a cough from the bedroom. So much for holding on to hope.

My wife's cough wasn't the only distressing sound I heard that day. Around noon, the disruption I had been expecting from outside began. It started with the revving of an engine. Someone was leaving their house.

I rolled over to the den window, certain the noise would be coming from the home of Josh, the young man who had mouthed off to the drone early that morning. I figured one of his houseguests was breaking quarantine in order to get back to their own home. I was wrong on that count.

When I got to the window and peeked through the blinds, I saw that it was Josh himself, and not a friend of his. My neighbor's party-boy son was at it again. I could see his driveway at the bottom of the cul-de-sac to the right of my house. I hardly noticed the black dandelions which had overtaken my lawn and the other lawns in the neighborhood. I was too interested in seeing someone doing what should have been a mundane thing but was now a breach of the newly implemented law.

He drove off, out of the cul-de-sac in his ostentatious cherry red Dodge Charger. It was a classic car from the 2010s, a gift from his parents and the only fully gas-powered vehicle on the block. Which meant the neighborhood always heard him and that big engine of his when he was coming or going. Watching him drive out of my field of vision, I was left to ponder what he could be leaving for. More importantly, I wanted to know how long it would take for him to be turned around and sent back home.

While I waited for the sound of Josh's engine to signify that he had returned, I listened out for the more disturbing sound of my wife coughing. She hadn't done so since the first time, and I was starting to hold out hope again.

Everything I had seen and read on the internet stated that there wasn't much that could be done at the hospitals. General antibiotics were being administered, rest and plenty of liquids were being recommended. As part of the Pandemic Prevention Response Plan, those exhibiting symptoms were encouraged to log on to the city website and request those general antibiotics. The medicine would be delivered to households throughout the country, eliminating the need to head to the hospital and the risk of increasing the spread of whatever this illness was. They also stressed that, while symptoms were severe, there was no reason to believe the illness was fatal. They turned out to be wrong about that too.

I was unreasonably nervous for Josh to return. I looked constantly from my various screens to the window and back again. On one of those screens, I logged on to the city website and made a request for antibiotics for my wife. It was a pretty straightforward process. I put in her name, our address, listed her symptoms, and received a message letting me know that the meds would be delivered within twenty-four hours. I had just completed the process when I heard the sound of an old-fashioned gas engine again.

It turned out it took fifteen minutes for Josh to come back home. I took some small, idiotic pleasure in knowing I had lasted out there, going from roadblock to roadblock, for at least twenty. I wondered for a moment if he might have been successful in whatever his mission was as I rolled to the window to take a look at what he was up to.

When my fingers separated the blinds, I could clearly see that his brief trip likely hadn't been a success. There was a chaser drone behind him. It hovered at the edge of his driveway, about six feet in the air, as Josh got out of the car.

He slammed the door so violently I lurched in my seat, feeling foolish for flinching as hard as I had. I was all nerves at this point. I was terrified about what was going on with my wife in the bedroom and I worried about what was going on with the outside world.

Josh was walking up the drive toward his front door when he whirled around and made me jump in my seat again. He screamed: "THIS IS SUPPOSED TO BE A FREE FUCKING COUNTRY!"

I tensed, waiting to see what the drone would say or do. I suppose Josh was waiting too, because he stood there, fists clenched and breathing hard. "People need FOOD! They need to WORK! We need to see DOCTORS, not just some fucking ANTIBIOTICS!" His voice was nearly shrill as he screamed at the drone.

I agreed with him on his last point, but other than a doctor, every essential item anyone needed could be delivered straight to our doors. We simply had to order our provisions online and they would be provided via drone or driverless delivery within the next day or two. Essential items (in Washington state, at least) even included marijuana and alcohol. I got the distinct feeling that whatever Josh had left the house for was something harder than either of those things. It was likely something he couldn't legally obtain. More than likely something he needed to keep his little party going hot throughout this quarantine.

The drone hung in the air, observing Josh. I interpreted this as a pause from the person manning

68

the chaser from whatever station they were in. The operator was likely looking up Josh on his or her system, seeing that another drone had already had an encounter with the young man early this morning.

After the pause, the electronic voice projected out to Josh and the rest of the neighborhood: "THIS IS YOUR SECOND WARNING, JOSHUA RAYSON OF 6 EAGLESTONE COURT. YOU WILL NOT BE WARNED AGAIN. FOLLOW THE RULES AND REGULATIONS OF THE PANDEMIC PREVENTION RESPONSE PLAN. ANOTHER ACT OF DEFIANCE, INCLUDING A BREACH OF QUARANTINE, WILL RESULT IN YOUR APPREHENSION."

"Apprehension?! For what? Breaching a fucking *quarantine*? This is America, asshole! Apprehend THIS!" He grabbed and thrusted his crotch again.

That insult of a gesture seemed to be the main tool in his arsenal. I can't lie, though, now that I wasn't in the crosshairs of the chaser, I found it a bit humorous. It was one of the few bits of levity to be had throughout this ordeal. But if I had known how it would all turn out, I would have felt dread in that moment instead of the ghoulish entertainment I was drawing from Josh's interaction with the drone. That makes me feel guilty as I write this now. But I didn't know, so I continued to watch and listen, feeling like a spectator at a show.

I was aware that I wasn't the only one who might have been peeking through blinds or watching from behind a barely drawn curtain. One of our other neighbors, Ben (who lived directly across from me but in a much larger house), was standing on the balcony of his house openly watching the whole thing.

The drone continued to hover there as if considering whether or not it would indeed apprehend the part of Josh he had suggested it do.

"RETURN TO YOUR HOME," the chaser projected, then it turned and zoomed off and away. I had a feeling it hadn't gone too far.

"Way to tell him, Josh! They can't violate our rights!" This came from Ben from across the street as he stood on his balcony which overlooked the half-circle of houses that made up the cul-de-sac that was Eaglestone Court. Our respective houses were on the ends of the horseshoe of five houses that made up our street.

Ben Stanton was a heavyset middle-aged man. That morning he was wearing shorts and a tank top. He rarely wore much more than that.

"Shut the fuck up, Ben!" Josh hollered. "No one cares what you think!"

Ben, an early retiree, wasn't particularly popular in our neighborhood. Before his retirement, he had been some sort of investor who had made several right moves (and never failed to brag about those moves as often as he could). He lived with his wife and two kids who were currently off at college. It wasn't the fact that he and his wife were snobs that rubbed the rest of the block the wrong way, it was that he had called the authorities on both Josh and his next-door neighbor, Jeanie. And that, in general, he was a dick.

He had called the police on Josh for being too loud on more than one occasion. In Jeanie's case, he had called the police when she'd hired a contractor to build a solarium at the back of her house. Ben had suspected she hadn't received a permit to build it, which she hadn't. Partway through the construction of the solarium, the project was shut down and Jeanie was out a lot more money before it could be continued.

On top of all of that, he always stared at my stumps. Most people glanced a time or two at my legs, and maybe a couple times more when they thought I wouldn't notice. I don't blame them for looking. By now I figured that was just part of human nature. I'm sure the sight of someone with no lower legs takes some getting used to. God knows it took me a long time to adjust to it as my new normal. However, people generally didn't gawk the way Ben did.

Each time I encountered him, his focus was on my legs. He spoke to me as though my thighs had eyes. I'm not sure if the guy has ever looked me in the face. Even worse, the first time we met (not long after he'd told me his name and delivered an oral biography on himself that I hadn't asked for) he'd had the nerve to say to me, while referring to my legs: "You lose those things in a war or something?" So, yeah, I wasn't shocked that Josh had responded to Ben the way he had, especially as angry as he was at the drone for stopping him from getting whatever it was he had breached quarantine to get.

Ben said nothing in response. I watched him slink from the balcony into his house. Again, I have to admit I laughed at this. He wasn't a nice man, and he had earned that response from Josh. Again, if I'd known how things would turn out for him, I might have cried instead.

I talked to Eunice for the rest of the evening. She had woken up feeling disoriented after having slept all day. She called out to me, screaming that she was blind. She had been blind for nearly a day now, so it surprised me that she was so surprised by this. I chalked it up to her waking up from a dream that had made her believe she could still see. But even after a few minutes awake, she remained confused. I sat out in the hallway, looking into our bedroom, feeling just as confused as she was. Eunice was saying things that didn't make sense to me.

She called me Mort, her ex-husband's name, and asked me to "Stop fucking screaming" at her when I called into the room asking if she was okay. When I went silent after that, she yelled out to me again, but this time by her son's name, Thomas. Then she began to cry. I didn't know what to do or say, except to remind her where she was, tell her who I was, and tell her how much I loved her.

The crying lasted a minute or so, and it seemed to clear her mind of her confusion. When she became coherent, she insisted that she have water. She was nearly hysterical in her demand for it. Confusion and feeling dehydrated were not any of the symptoms I had read or heard about. The edge and desperation in her voice frightened me, but once I brought her water she calmed down.

I entered the room holding my breath even though I had a mask (and swimming goggles) on. I was pushing a book cart from the den in front of me. I had emptied it of the books I had been planning to read next and placed a serving tray on top. On the tray were two thirty-two-ounce reusable water bottles along with a box of crackers. Attempting to keep some distance between us, I nudged the bed with the cart and let her know what I'd brought her. She sat up and felt for the items on top of the tray, eventually picking up one of the bottles of water. She drank it greedily, as though parched.

She downed both of the bottles within thirty seconds. I nearly forgot to roll out of the room because of how impressive a sight it was. But I did roll out, all the way to the kitchen, where I got a jug of filtered water from the fridge and brought it back to the room. I emptied it into the water bottles as Eunice sat and waited, her body language speaking of impatience.

She drank most of that as well. She thanked me, and I was thankful that she seemed more like herself after consuming all that water. I wondered how long it would be before I would need to lead her to the bathroom in order for that water to exit her system.

I rolled out into the hallway, where we could chat from a safe distance. We talked about nearly everything other than her condition. As always, she remained positive the entire time. I was just relieved that she was coherent and calm again.

We reminisced about better times and worse times. We still talked about our vacation plans. We discussed a trip to the Seattle Space Needle, and a visit to Pike Place Market to watch a few fish get chucked around before those iconic spots were closed down for good when Seattle retracted. It sounds impossible, but we even laughed while she lay there with something growing out of her eyes and attacking her body. That was what had always made us connect and stay connected, we had never had a problem cutting out the rest of the world and just enjoying one another. We talked until both of us fell asleep, I'm not certain which one of us went first.

It was because of the party at the bottom of the street that I eventually woke up.

Wednesday, May 3, 2045

"TURN THAT GODDAMN MUSIC DOWN! SOME OF US ARE TRYING TO SLEEP!"

It was Ben yelling from across the street. He had been shouting for some time, but those were the words I remember hearing first when I woke up. I could barely hear the music that he was complaining about. There was the faint sound of a guitar riff in the otherwise silent night. I suppose Ben thought his loud and grating voice was the lesser of two evils when he decided to scream out from his balcony. The man was insufferable.

From the hallway where I had fallen asleep, I could hear my wife breathing loudly and evenly from inside the room. I was relieved that Ben hadn't woken her.

I checked my phone and saw that the time was just after two in the morning. I also saw a slew of push notifications featuring headlines related to what no one was yet willing to label as a pandemic. With measures still being widely referred to as a "Preventative Shutdown."

After quickly scrolling through the headlines, and not feeling particularly hopeful about what they had to say, I decided to watch the show going on outside.

Ordering the lights on in the den, I listened to the ruckus coming from outside as I moved toward the den window. Ben was still crying for Josh to keep it down. In response, Josh had pumped the music louder, but not before yelling out to Ben to "Shut the fuck up" for the second time in less than twenty-four hours.

I got to the window and peered through the blinds, seeing that Ben was leaning over the balcony on the second storey of his house, as I expected him to be. He was twisting his torso toward Josh's house and the sound of the music. I worried for a second that he might fall over the railing with the way he was stretched out from it, shaking his fist in a cartoonish fury as Josh continued to play his music. Even though it was a second storey balcony, it would have been a long drop onto a hard surface. It made me nervous watching him lean out the way he was.

Ben's response to being told to shut up was to yell, as loud as a bullhorn: "YOUR PARENTS OUGHT TO BE ASHAMED RAISING A LITTLE PIECE OF SHIT LIKE YOU! IT'S NO WONDER THEY'RE GONE ALL THE TIME!"

I tensed at that. I truly hoped the music was too loud for Josh to hear what Ben had said. The kid had a temper, the neighborhood knew it. There had been more than one occasion when he and his parents had fought loudly enough for all to hear. Their last blow up had been just before their most recent trip. That had been a fight right on the driveway as Josh was helping them load up their luggage. Not long after they had left, he'd had a spat with his girlfriend on nearly the same spot.

Witnessing situations like that was one of the good and bad things about working from home; I got to see and hear a lot of what the neighbors were up to when they didn't think people were around, even things I'd rather not see and hear. But not only were people around at this moment, they were on edge. Ben wasn't doing anything to help the situation.

In addition to my house and Josh's, the lights were on at the house between Josh and Ben's place, where Jeanie lived. I was certain she was witnessing the show discreetly, as I was. The only one of the five houses on the block with the lights off was the one I couldn't see from my vantage at the window of my den. My next-door neighbors were snowbirds, though the term wasn't technically accurate. It rarely snowed in Seattle in the winter, but it was incredibly rainy. The retired couple next to me, Leslie and Ashley George, spent most of those rainy winters in Mexico. They generally left after Halloween and came back in late May. Eunice checked on their house from time to time to make sure everything was in order. Before they got back each spring, Josh would often mow their lawns and make sure things were tidy for their arrival. He had been doing that for them since he was a teen. I believe he was a good kid at heart. A good kid who likely could have used more structure for most of his life. On this night, however, there would be nothing good coming from Josh after what Ben had called out.

Josh's music was abruptly turned off. Everything went quiet. I looked out there and could almost see the tension building between Josh's house and Ben's. The streetlights and the house lights illuminated the semicircle of a street, causing it to almost seem like a stage as the altercation escalated.

I looked over at Ben when Josh's music cut off. I couldn't see his face clearly, though his body language made me think he took the silence as a victory. I think he thought his yelling had worked. I was worried about the opposite. And I was right.

Enter stage right, Joshua Rayson, angsty rich kid on edge. He came out of the house with a hockey stick in his hands. He was barely onto his walkway before he yelled out: "What the fuck did you say about my parents, old man?"

From his body language, his overall tone, and the speed with which he was crossing the little bit of road that would get him to Ben's house, I guessed this was a rhetorical question. Josh wasn't looking for any sort of conversation even though he repeated his question again: "What the fuck did you say?"

Josh was nearly six-feet tall and made of lean muscle. He had decided to show off that muscle. He was walking to Ben's house shirtless, wearing only a pair of jogging pants and sneakers. He reminded me of me during my athletic days prior to my accident. I saw the knucklehead I used to be as I watched him stride toward Ben's place.

Ben seemed to have no interest in repeating what he had said about Josh's parents, and I didn't blame him. Instead of answering Josh, he provided the neighborhood with new information: "I'M SICK! I'M SICK! STAY AWAY! I JUST WANT TO REST AND GET BETTER! STAY AWAY! HELP!"

I wasn't sure if he was telling the truth or if this was a cowardly ploy to keep Josh from climbing his house like King Kong and feeding him that hockey stick. Either way, he was nearly jumping up and down on his balcony in fear as he watched the kid approach his home.

I almost felt sorry for Ben, except I remembered all the shitty things he had done, and his judgmental stares and snide remarks. I resented him for waking me up a few minutes before all this. I also resented the fact that he could have woken my wife, who seemed to be in far worse shape than he was if he was sick with the same thing she had. I was nearly rooting for Josh to silence him however he could. But after looking carefully at Josh, I hoped the boy wouldn't go too far.

By the time Josh got to Ben's lawn I was expecting him to sprint to the door and run right through it. The kid didn't look right. It wasn't just that he sounded crazed or that he was bare-chested and banging his chest, or even that he was carrying a hockey stick he seemed intent on using. It was the way he was walking. Nearly a soldier's march. A straight line from his home to Ben's. He looked absolutely determined to get himself locked up at Ben's expense.

Ben continued to yell as he watched Josh tread his lawn from his perch on his balcony. It was only when Ben stopped responding in sentences and started to repeatedly cry out for help that I snapped out of the trance I'd been put under by watching something potentially dangerous unfold, experiencing some variant of the bystander effect.

I snapped out of it and reached for my phone, which was resting on my lap. I pressed 9 and 1. I did not want to call the police on Josh, but despite how much of an asshole Ben had been to many of us, I didn't want to see him murdered. I also didn't want to see Josh's future dead along with Ben. I considered going out there and attempting to calm Josh down; he and I had always gotten along well. But I had no intention of putting myself in immediate danger when

Josh was this angry. More importantly, I didn't want to risk leaving Eunice alone.

I watched Josh walk up the lawn, onto the flagstone walkway that led to a flagstone patio beneath the balcony, and then to the door. I told myself that I would press the last digit if Josh intended to break into Ben's house. It seemed as though that was how it was going to go.

He was on the walkway, still marching in that militant way toward the door. My hand hovered above the button that would send the police there. I thought back to the deployment drone threatening to apprehend Josh if he committed another infraction, including breaching quarantine as he was doing right now. I doubted the police would approve of breaking and entering as well as assault in addition to the breaching of quarantine offense.

I didn't want to press the final digit, but as he got closer to the door, I knew that I would have to. And I would have pressed the second 1 if not for the third voice that called out into the street.

"Hey! Both of you! I have two young girls in here that are sick with whatever this is that's going around, and they're acting more maturely than you are. Josh: the music is a bit too loud. Ben: yelling about it to the entire neighborhood isn't going to help. PLEASE, for the sake of my kids, can you both just NOT do this right now? Aren't things bad enough?"

It was Jeanie Morneau, who owned the house to the right of Ben's and to the left of Josh's from my vantage point; she lived between the two. I was thankful she was there between the two at that moment. She was the most respected person in our little neighborhood, and she was standing on her front porch in a robe, not sounding very happy with her two neighbors.

Jeanie was a single mother of two. She had divorced an abuser, successfully sued him, and wound up in this cul-de-sac. That wasn't why she was the most respected person in this grouping of houses, however. She was respected because of what had happened when her ex-husband had shown up here, breaking his restraining order and threatening to take his two daughters from their mother.

The man had been crazed; it had been just after ten in the morning. I know because I had been by my den window then, too. Except, on that morning, I had pressed the second 1 on my phone and asked for the police to show up. It turned out Jeanie hadn't needed them.

When her husband had begun banging on her door, threatening her for all to hear, she had opened her door with a gun in her hand, pointing it at the man's chest. He had quieted a great deal after that. He'd stayed quiet as she'd kept the gun trained on him, backing him down and keeping him on the lawn until the police had shown up. Eunice had immediately gained a great deal of respect and admiration for Jeanie after hearing about the incident with the gun, wishing she could have done the same to her ex-husband to save her child. The two had become fast friends after that.

It might have been that gun and that incident that Josh was thinking about as he froze in the middle of his march toward Ben's front door. Ben stopped shouting as well. The neighborhood was quiet again until Jeanie said: "If we're going to make it through this thing, we're going to have to work together. *Please* guys, things are bad enough as they are."

Josh paused on the patio just as my finger paused over the 1 button on my phone. I was waiting to see what he would do, hoping he would turn around. I didn't want to call the police, especially if it meant Ben would make Josh look like he had started this all even though the kid wouldn't have left his house if Ben hadn't hit him where he was obviously most vulnerable in mentioning his parents.

I thought back to when Josh had tried to leave earlier and wondered if what he hadn't been able to obtain on his short breach of quarantine then was playing into his behavior at that moment. Maybe what he had left for was something that might have mellowed him out. In the absence of whatever that thing might have been, Jeanie's voice was seemingly having the calming effect Josh needed. He said: "Sorry about that, Ms. M."

I wasn't sure if he stopped because her statement had returned him to his senses, or because he was picturing the same revolver she had used to stand down her ex-husband. I would never know. I suspected it was a bit of both. If anyone on the street was equipped to handle the hostilities that this sort of situation might bring, it was Jeanie Morneau.

"Thank you, Jeanie! I'm glad there's *someone* trying to be reasonable during this mess!" Ben called down from the balcony.

"Give it a rest, Ben! You're not the only one suffering here. Screaming out into the street about everything you're upset about isn't helping anyone!"

"Yeah, Ben. Give it a rest," Josh said, though I barely heard it. He wasn't yelling anymore. He looked calm. As calm as someone who had been as frenzied as he had been just moments before could look. It seemed like he was ready to return home, but he had one more small insult to send Ben's way. This one wouldn't require any words.

With his hockey stick, he batted one of the lawn gnomes on Ben's yard, sending the little elf cartwheeling across the grass. Josh, in his quiet fury, didn't seem bothered by the dandelion fluff that kicked into the air and floated toward him on the light wind still leftover from the most recent windstorm.

I was certain it was landing all over the exposed skin of his torso. Thinking of the rash that had developed on my wife's face and hands after her run through the windblown dandelion fluff only a few days earlier, I didn't envy the position Josh was putting himself in. No one in any official capacity had linked the dandelions to the illness that was going around, but I felt it was too coincidental not to be connected. I prayed Josh wouldn't end up suffering like my wife was due to Ben goading him on.

I watched Ben prepare himself to bark from his balcony over the use of his lawn ornament for slapshot practice. Just as it seemed like he was going to scream out again, he looked over in the direction of Jeanie's house and appeared to think better of it. Instead, he turned back and headed through the door that led to the master bedroom of his house, slamming it shut behind him. The noise echoed in the wind like a gunshot. And, like a gunshot, it sent everyone dispersing. Jeanie went back into her home after firing Josh an exasperated glance as he cut the short distance across the street on his way back to his house.

I watched to see if he might turn around, run back and start swatting away at the rest of Ben's lawn ornaments, but he went home quietly and, seemingly, calmly. This time there were three of his guests waiting in front of his house to greet him.

I didn't trust the calm I sensed from Josh. It reminded me of the false calm before a raging storm. I couldn't help but wonder when that storm would break and hit our neighborhood.

Headlines from May 3, 2045. All over the internet, people were arguing over what was really going on. The only certainty was confusion

From Read Between the Lies:

BLACK DANDELIONS A SIGN OF THE END OF THE WORLD!

From The Daphnis Daily Herald:

Cause For Optimism As New Disease Is Given Name And Classification

From The Unmitigated Truth:

Black Dandelions and new Illness are the Result of Chinese Biological Weaponry: World War Imminent

From the World Health Organization:

Development of vaccine underway as new contagion identified as variant of old disease

The vibration of my phone woke me up. I had fallen asleep at my desk while on the computer after the altercation between Josh and Ben. My phone was on the table, the vibration jolted through me like an electric pulse. I checked it immediately, wondering if it was another emergency alert. It turned out it was a notification stating that the medication had been delivered; the antibiotics that were meant to fight off whatever was attacking my wife's system were here.

Before heading to the door, I checked my go-to news app and saw that not much had changed. We were still under pandemic preventative lockdown. Hospitals were still at capacity with the patients who had made it there and checked in before the lockdown had been announced.

At that point, there was no new word on treatment. The recommendation was still fluids and the meds they were sending around to those on drug plans or who could afford them. People were still being advised to stay away from anyone infected, and to stay indoors at all costs. The disease seemed to be airborne and aggressive.

There was one newly reported piece of information regarding symptoms that wasn't particularly new news to me: the disease seemed to attack the skin, causing what they were describing as a rash or skin discoloration. I thought of the blemishes on my wife's face and hands. She had been covered up everywhere else when she'd gone on her run. I had already figured out that that couldn't have been a coincidence. I suspected that whatever it was that was getting into people's systems and making them sick was likely making them sick from the outside as well.

With that in mind, I put on a mask, my goggles, a pair of biodegradable reusable nitrile gloves, and a rain jacket before I went to the front porch to collect the package left there by delivery drone.

Delivery drones had become commonplace over the last decade. I was more thankful for them at that moment than ever before. I had previously been one of many who had lamented the loss of thousands of jobs due to the mechanization of delivery, but in a situation like this, the autonomous automobiles and delivery drone systems were absolutely essential.

While I was out on the porch retrieving the package, I heard a door open somewhere on the block. It turned out to be Ben's wife, Gloria. The plump, middle-aged woman was reaching for a package on the ground but seemed to be struggling. I noticed that she was holding on to the porch railing with a delicacy I had never seen from her before. It took me a moment to realize that she was feeling her way to the package almost as much as she was freely moving toward it. I remembered my wife complaining that it looked like a film had been placed over her eyes before she had gone blind.

I heard another door open and saw Ben emerge on the balcony above and to the left of Gloria.

It was nearly nine in the morning and the sun was shining bright. I realized I hadn't paid much attention to the weather reports since hearing of the recent windstorms. But, thinking about it that morning, I noted that it hadn't rained in over a week. That was highly unusual for spring in the Pacific Northwest. It was just one more odd event in a series of them.

The wind was still swirling, though it wasn't as violent as it had been when Eunice had gone out for her run. Spores and seeds and pollen were in the air, floating around, waiting to land and infect. That's what I believed anyway. The mainstream news hadn't come out and said it, but it was clear (to me at least) that the dandelions had brought this. I thought of a few of the conspiracy headlines I had read in the last few days:

BLACK DANDELIONS A SIGN OF THE END OF THE WORLD

WORLDWIDE WINDSTORMS CONTROLLED BY THE GOVERNMENT AS POPULATION REDUCTION PROJECT UNDERWAY

BLACK DANDELIONS A BIOENGINEERING EXPERIMENT GONE WRONG

PILLS SENT BY THE GOVERNMENT ARE THE FIRST STEP IN THEIR PLAN TO CONTROL OUR MINDS

I dismissed the notion of government mind control outright. That was one of the laughable conspiracies (and one of the scary ones too, considering that people actually believed it). I didn't think it was the government controlling the weather either, but I thought the weather odd enough to believe that something out of the norm was going on. I understood that whatever was going on had to be related to the black dandelions, which I had considered to be a bad sign from the beginning. They were turning white, spreading their seeds, and popping up again at an alarming rate. The black weeds were on every lawn all over the neighborhood, but it wasn't the dandelions I was focused on that morning. I was focused on Ben on his balcony.

In the light of the sun, I saw that he hadn't been lying earlier that morning when he had warned Josh that he was sick. Much like his wife, he was not doing well. He was wearing what were likely the same singlet and shorts as he had been wearing since at least the previous day. Now that the sun was out, I could see the dark red-brown blotches all over his arms and legs even from across the street. It looked like someone had taken a boat paddle to his body, leaving it badly bruised. He was squinting down at his wife just as she was squinting down at the packages delivered to their home. Both of them were sick. Both were going blind. Seeing this, I vowed to not take off my goggles until this thing was over.

I took our delivery into the house, hoping to God that the medication would make some difference for my neighbors and, more importantly, for Eunice.

"More water, please," Eunice said after I carefully brought her the medication that had just been delivered. Her voice was a rasp. She had just downed three thirty-two-ounce bottles of water but sounded as though she hadn't had a drink in days. Her eyes were completely sealed over by whatever had begun to grow there. It was green, thick, and reminded me of the film of algae that grows on the bottom of a creek. I nearly cried at the sight of her, but I put a smile in my voice and told her that things would get better. I hoped I sounded more optimistic than I felt.

I gave her one of the antibiotic pills and more water, making sure to wear nitrile gloves each time I made contact with her. Like Ben, the skin on her face and hands was still covered with red-brown splotches. I did my best not to focus on her eyes or the rash and tried to put my faith in the medication I had just given her. I collected the bottles she had emptied and turned immediately to get more water, only turning back when I heard her cough.

It was the first time she had coughed since yesterday. This cough sounded much worse. It was harsh and racking; it seemed to be coming from deep in her chest. I looked toward her and almost wished I hadn't. I was going to ask her if she was okay, but I wasn't able to form the words. Besides, the answer was obvious.

The room was dim, the blinds were down and closed. The only source of light was coming from the lamp on the nightstand beside the bed. Because of the poor lighting I wondered if maybe my eyes were playing tricks on me. I desperately wished they were, but I knew that I had seen what I thought I had seen.

Eunice lay on her back, coughing. With each cough, something was coming out of her. At first, I thought it was spittle or phlegm, but what was spraying out of her floated in the air over her body and the bed. The discharge only drifted in the air for a few moments, but to me it looked like dandelion fluff blowing on a puff of air or gust of wind. The spittle (whatever it was) slowly drifted to the bed.

Her coughing stopped, and she looked at me pleadingly. I should say, rather, that she faced me. She couldn't exactly look at me because her eyes were entirely covered over by green growth by that point.

She asked for more water as she tried to recover from the coughing spell. I turned and went to get the water for her, not wanting to think of what she might have just coughed up. Again, I prayed the antibiotics would work.

I must have brought Eunice three gallons of water by the evening. The experts were all advising that those suffering would require plenty of fluids while dealing with this contagion. As for food, however, no advice was given. I had tried to get her to eat chicken noodle soup, but even the smell of it put a look on her face that said she would throw up if she went any closer to it. I asked her if she thought she could at least try to hold some of it down. She simply shook her head, making a disgusted face in the direction of the soup as it sat on the book cart in front of her. She seemed to shrink into the bedding in repulsion of it. I took the soup away, along with the crackers I had brought her the previous day. She hadn't touched those either.

Next, I brought her orange juice, hopeful that the always recommended vitamin C would do her some good. As I had with the water and the soup, I placed the glass of orange juice on the book cart, which was now doubling as a mobile serving tray, and pushed it toward her bed, making sure to keep a safe distance away.

Each time I entered the room, I remembered the fluff she had coughed up earlier. I was still wearing my goggles and mask, feeling foolish but too scared to care. She struggled to sit up but managed to.

Eunice took a hesitant sip of the orange juice. I waited to see if she would throw it up or push it away. She seemed to play with the taste in her mouth before swallowing, as though she had never experienced that particular liquid before. Seeming to approve of it, she downed the juice as readily as she had the water, and that relieved me. What she said after emptying the glass struck me as unusual, however. Her voice was still raspy and strained as she struggled to string together a few short sentences: "More, please... Add sugar. Lots of sugar."

After a few glasses of orange juice loaded with sugar, and another half gallon of water, Eunice went back to sleep. It was just after eight in the evening when I went back to the den. I continued to watch the live stream of the news. I was expecting to hear what I had heard all day: reports of an emergency lockdown and the strict enforcement of it, but no clue given as to how long the lockdown would last; descriptions of the illness and hospitals that were full to the brim with patients suffering from it, but no word on how to solve it.

I was pleasantly surprised when I heard a bit of different, more positive news: scientists had not only identified the disease, but they had given it several names rather than just calling it a "mysterious contagion" as they had since this started.

The Rubivirus was the first and most popular name I saw and read in the news. Then there was the World Health Organization's designation of it as RUVID-45 (for Rubivirus Disease 2045 – named for the year this variant of the disease was discovered). Others were simply calling it Hyper Rubella. What all those names meant was that the scientists working hard to figure this all out were comfortable enough to call it a hyperaggressive, mutated version of rubella.

As you can probably imagine, I (and a ton of others around the world, I'm sure) spent most of that evening researching rubella. It was a disease I had heard of before, but nothing I had given much thought to. I hadn't had to think about it because the MMR vaccine was something most people in most of the world had been given as children since the 1960s. It had successfully protected those inoculated with it against measles, mumps and rubella for decades, which made this outbreak particularly perplexing. From everything I read, however, the diagnosis of rubella (or something rubella related) made logical sense. The symptoms were largely the same: fever, headache, runny nose and cough; most importantly, the pink eye and red rash all over the skin.

The fact that they were able to identify the virus family that this new disease belonged to, and the fact that it was a disease that already had a vaccine, were supposed to be positive things. It meant a vaccine would be on the way soon. Viewers were told that one was already under development. It was expected to be rolled out in a matter of weeks. In the meanwhile, because of the severity of the symptoms, especially the blindness (which I was relieved to hear scientists hoped would be temporary), the strict lockdown would have to remain in effect.

It was the same on every news station and mainstream website. Reasons for optimism were spreading. I was catching that optimism willingly. I had to be positive as I thought of Eunice cowering from the soup and crackers I had offered her. I pictured her shaking, burning hot, her eyes sealed over by this new version of an old disease, sometimes disoriented, and barely able to speak in complete sentences. What choice did I have but to be optimistic?

I might have stayed optimistic if not for what happened next.

It was around 9:00 PM when it happened. I was having a late meal. Some sort of microwavable dinner. Frozen Salisbury steak, green beans, and mashed potatoes; each of which tasted nothing like the food they were declared to be. They tasted instead like variations of cardboard, which was fine with me. I didn't have much of an appetite.

As I was finishing my meal at my desk, I wondered how long it had been since I'd last eaten. It might have been early that morning; it might have been the night before. Time was sort of blending together in that way that is unique to being locked inside your house for days.

I also felt guilty to be eating, as silly as that sounds. Eunice hadn't eaten a proper meal in days.

Not since coming back from her run on Sunday, and I don't think she'd had much even then.

She didn't seem to be going to the bathroom either. Even with all the water she was taking in, I hadn't heard the toilet being used or flushed once. And as far as I could tell, she wasn't pissing in the bed. The only fluid that left her was in the form of strange, earthy, almost sweet-smelling sweat. That worried me even more than the lack of eating.

As I was thinking of how to get something nutritious into my wife, I heard the sound from outside that ruined my optimism and set this whole situation on a further downward spiral I couldn't have predicted. It was the sound of a vehicle.

I barely heard the engine before the sound of peeling tires overtook it. A car was skidding to a stop. I went to the window, knowing what to expect and not being surprised when I saw what I saw. It was Josh again. I must have missed the sound of him leaving when I was heating up my food or checking on Eunice, but it was him. He was returning from another errand that likely couldn't be easily explained to the authorities.

As I watched his car idling there in his driveway, I wondered if the chaser drone hovering behind it, flashing its blue and red lights, would bother to ask him for an explanation.

Josh cut the engine and bounced out of his car. He didn't seem to have anything in his hands, at least not until he turned toward the chaser drone and filled both of his hands with his crotch. He once again thrust his groin in the direction of the chaser. He didn't say anything this time, nothing that I could hear, anyway. But I could easily imagine him saying "Apprehend THIS" again.

I couldn't hear him laugh, though his body language and facial expression suggested that was what he was doing. He was laughing at the drone. He continued to laugh as he removed his hands from his crotch and gave the hovering orb both of his middle fingers. He then walked calmly to his house. Two of the partiers who had fallen into quarantine with him (a guy and a girl) waited for him at the door. The guy gave him a high five as he met them. They entered the house, laughing and saying things I couldn't quite make out.

After Josh's front door was closed, I expected the drone to fly off as the two previous chasers had done before it. To my growing discomfort, it only continued to hover there under the glow of the streetlights. Its flashing lights cut off all at once, making the drone more difficult to see. But I saw it, and I watched it, because something was starting to tell me that it wasn't done there.

I wish I could say for sure how long I sat there watching that drone, but the longer I watched, the more it felt like time was behaving strangely. It felt like seconds were taking longer than they should to pass. It seemed like time was slowing way down. I knew I was waiting for something, even though I wasn't sure what. The wait felt like it took an eternity, and then, when the wait was over, what happened next seemed like it was happening at double speed. At least that's how it felt. Isn't that always how it goes when you're waiting for something terrible to occur?

I barely saw them until they were parked. There were no sirens. There were no flashing lights. The two vehicles that had pulled onto the street were big but moved silently. The first was one of the many black SUVs I had seen at the roadblocks where I had first learned of the quarantine. The other looked like an ambulance, except it was mostly yellow aside from a band of white and red stripes along the bottom panel. Even from a distance and in the dark, I could see the words **HAZARDOUS TRANSPORT** written on the side of it. Beneath that was the universal symbol for a biohazard.

Four soldiers in HAZMAT suits (who looked identical to the ones who had turned Eunice and I around at those intersections on the first day of the quarantine) hopped out of the vehicles; one out of the passenger side of the yellow ambulance, the other three out of the SUV. All of them carried assault weapons. Each of them was pointing their very large guns at Joshua's house. They approached it swiftly and methodically.

In what felt like mere moments, it was over. The only sounds made the entire time came from Josh's front door when the leading soldier kicked it to splinters, and a few shouts of protest from inside which were very quickly cut short. I hate to imagine what might have silenced the people in the house so quickly. Officers have all sorts of methods to stun and silence people these days. I was just thankful not to have heard any gunshots.

Quickly, three of the soldiers exited the house. One was in the lead pointing his weapon ahead of him as if expecting some sort of ambush. The other two each emerged from the house carrying bodies, their guns strapped to their backs as they moved Josh and his guests out of his home.

The soldier who was dragging a limp Josh had him from beneath the armpits. Josh's shoeless heels were scraping against the ground. His hands were bound in front of him, and he didn't seem to be offering any resistance.

The soldier who followed had a girl slung over his shoulder and was dragging a young man behind him by his bound wrists, seemingly unbothered that he was scraping the boy's shirtless back against the grass of Josh's lawn, right through the dandelions. That same boy was then dragged over the sidewalk and the asphalt of the street.

The soldiers loaded these three into the back of the hazardous transport vehicle. The three soldiers stopped long enough to look back toward the house in unison. They were waiting for the same thing I was waiting for: the fourth soldier.

He exited the house not long after the rest had. He was carrying a small body, the sex of which I couldn't identify, in his arms. It was someone who had likely been in a different part of the house when his or her friends had been ambushed. This person was quickly reunited with those same friends as they were shoved into the back of the biohazard vehicle.

The soldiers returned to their respective spots in the two vehicles and drove off as quickly and quietly as they had arrived. The drone hovered there for a moment longer, then rose higher in the air before following the vehicles.

If I had gone to the bathroom for five minutes, I would have missed it all. Although Ben would have caught me up pretty quickly.

When the vehicles and drone were out of sight, I heard my obnoxious neighbor shout out from his balcony: "THIS IS HOW IT HAPPENS! THIS IS WHAT THEY DO! FIRST THEY GIVE US THIS DISEASE AND LEAVE US TO ROT, THEN THEY COME AND TAKE US AWAY TO DO EXPERIMENTS AND TESTS AND GOD KNOWS WHAT. THIS IS HOW IT STARTS, YOU HEAR ME? THEY'RE GOING TO RUIN US ALL!"

I hadn't seen him during the entire ordeal. I had been too focused on what was going on at Josh's house. But now I saw him there, standing on his balcony in his underwear in the dark. I wasn't sure who he was talking to, and I wasn't sure that he was sure either. If his condition was progressing at the same rate my wife's had, he should have been at least half blind, and likely disoriented. It was a surprise he could see what had happened, just as much as it was a surprise that he had the strength to be on his balcony bellowing.

While Ben continued to rant and rave, I returned to the living room and turned on the TV. The news was still playing. I turned it up loud enough to nearly drown out the already faint sound of Ben's shouting. I wasn't listening to what was being said by the reporters on my screen, I only wanted the noise. Whatever it was they were talking about, I'm sure it had nothing to do with military types showing up to suburban neighborhoods in the night and abducting a group of kids.

I went to my kitchen, attempting to come to terms with what I had seen while part of me was trying to convince myself that I hadn't just seen it. I went to the cabinet where we keep our liquor, beer, and wine. We had plenty of each, though I wondered for the first time if we would have to order more before all of this was said and done.

Thinking of Josh and his friends being dragged out of his house, I poured myself a finger of scotch and shot it like tequila. Then poured and swallowed another two shots. I considered putting the bottle back in the cabinet, then reconsidered. I took the bottle and the glass and put them on my lap. After checking in on Eunice, who was sleeping soundly (I hoped that was a sign of recovery), I went back to the den.

I opened my laptop, and that's when I decided to write this document. I decided to type it all out just in case. Because it was then I truly started to worry that not all of us would make it out of this alive.

Headlines from May 4, 2045

From Read Between the Lies:

SCIENTISTS ARE LYING ABOUT SO CALLED 'HYPER RUBELLA'

From ABC News:

Experts Hopeful RUVID-45 Vaccines Will Get Full FDA Approval Within Week

From The Unmitigated Truth:

Government Plotting to Reduce the Population After Global Warming and Pollution Concerns Worsen

Government Task Force Abducting and Experimenting on Those who are Afflicted

From The Seattle Times:

Doctors Hopeful As Reports From Hospitalized Patients Show Marked Improvement In Strength And Cognition After Days Of Being Infected With RUVID-45

Thursday, May 4, 2045

While putting this document together, I spent hours searching the web. I looked up articles and videos both from well respected news entities all over the world and from the conspiratorial corners of the internet. I saw articles that mostly confirmed and regurgitated what was being said on the news: RUVID-45 was dangerous, if not deadly, and was considered highly contagious.

There was promising news about a potential improvement in patients' energy and state of mind after days of battling the disease and facing the weakness and disorientation (along with the other host of symptoms) it caused. As with rubella, the professionals were now saying that bedrest and medication for fever should lead to recovery; though with this new form of the illness, that recovery would more than likely take a while longer than the three days to a week it takes to shake off standard rubella. The most promising news was that a vaccine was likely just around the corner. Unfortunately, there was no word about a cure. Despite that, I had reason to feel hopeful. Not only because of the positive news but because of Eunice herself.

Like the hospitalized patients the news mentioned, she seemed to have experienced an increase in her strength this morning when I went to check on her. Her voice was coming back, and she had spoken to me in full sentences for the first time in days.

Her eyes, unfortunately, were still clotted over with that green growth I was starting to think of as moss. Other than that, I had to consider her recent improvements as an indication that she was on the road to recovery.

Also in the news was ongoing debate about the tactics governments worldwide were using regarding the extreme lockdowns. Most seemed to be in agreement that the radical measures were necessary. At least that was what was being said in the traditional news media, which wasn't the case on the conspiracy sites I couldn't help visiting. On those sites, I saw all matter of concerning things. While I realize that concerning people is the nature and main purpose of most conspiracy sites, after what had happened to Josh, and after Ben's raving rant that followed, I couldn't help but to be drawn to some of the headlines. Particularly:

Government Plotting to Reduce the Population After Global Warming and Pollution Concerns Worsen

And:

Government Task Force Abducting and Experimenting on Those who are Afflicted

These had popped up after I'd typed "military response to RUVID" into the search engine, hoping to find out more information in general. I also wanted to know what protocol might have led to Josh and his friends being apprehended. I had called the police not long after they had been taken, and I'd gotten no helpful information. I'd gotten no information at all. The internet was my only recourse.

In the article about government abductions and experimentation, I saw a photo of a black SUV and yellow ambulance parked on a street that could have been mine or any other in suburban America. There were several photos of this sort from several different locations. I felt foolish for not even considering recording or photographing what I had witnessed happen to Josh. I'd been too shocked and absorbed in what I'd been seeing to do anything but stare.

I was in the middle of reading the article when a phone call came in, the unexpected sound of which nearly caused me to have a heart attack. I wasn't too surprised by who it was. I figured it would only be a matter of time before we spoke given what had happened on our street so far. I answered the phone and said hello to Jeanie Morneau from across the road.

"Hi, Alex. How are you and Eunice doing?"

I sighed into the phone, wondering how best to answer. I was optimistic after the new medical reports, but my wife was still laying in bed, blind and hoping for the best. "She's not so great. But as of this morning she seemed a bit stronger than she was yesterday. I still seem to be symptom free, thank God. How about you? How are you and the girls?"

It was her turn to sigh before letting me know that her girls, Daisy and Rose, were also not great but seemed to be heading in the right direction. Her two daughters couldn't see, but this morning they had regained some of their strength. They were begging for candy like crazy and she couldn't help but feed it to them. It was all they would eat. I let her know that Eunice was much the same, constantly asking for sugar. We both agreed that must be a positive thing. After an awkward pause, she said: "I need you to tell me I'm not going crazy."

"I don't think that's something I can do, Jeanie, considering everything that's going on. I'm not so sure of my own sanity." She laughed a bit at that, though she did so like someone who wasn't accustomed to making the sound. As meek as it sounded, I couldn't recall many times in life when I had appreciated hearing laughter more. It had been scarce over the last few days.

At the same time, we both said: "Did you see what happened to Josh?"

She had whispered it, as if worried someone might be able to overhear us. I guess I wasn't the only one feeling conspiratorial that morning. I let her know that I had indeed seen what had happened. She sounded relieved at that, saying: "Good. Because I just got off the phone with the police, and they say there's no record of Josh being arrested. Not at any of the stations in the county, according to the person who searched his name."

"I'm not surprised. I called a couple of precincts last night." I didn't mention that I had been half in the bag when I'd done so, the scotch giving me the courage to make the calls. What I did say was: "When I actually *could* get through, I got the same answer you did. I thought maybe it was too early to check. But when I tried again this morning, the response was the same. I've been looking up military responses to the pandemic for the last little bit since then."

"Ah, okay... At least I know I'm not going crazy... Thank you. Have you found anything that makes sense?" It almost seemed as though she didn't want to ask the question. But she also sounded desperate for any kind of answer, just like I was.

"Don't worry. I haven't gotten to Ben's level of paranoia, but there are things online that I would have thought were crazy until I saw what happened to Josh. To be honest, I never even would have thought we'd be in a forced lockdown like this, so I don't know what to believe anymore. The pandemic twenty years ago was bad, but this... I feel like it's worse than they're letting on. And that's hard to imagine."

She told me that she agreed, then she said: "What do you think *is* going on?"

I had no idea. I let her know as much before saying: "I'll send you the link I'm looking at. You can tell me if I'm crazy for even clicking on it."

I put her on hold after she agreed to look at the article about people being abducted by the government. I'd been reading it on my laptop. I tried to search for the link on my phone so I could send it to her while we were on the line, but I couldn't find it. I couldn't find anything. I felt sick to my stomach as I saw what came up when I searched for the article. The words on my screen read: **THERE IS NO INTERNET SERVICE AVAILABLE**.

I swore and had to apologize to Jeanie as soon as the word left my mouth. I told her: "I think the internet is down."

"No way. I was just on it," she responded. I told her I had been, too. I refreshed the site on my laptop and saw essentially the same message on the screen: **THERE IS NO INTERNET SERVICE.** Beneath this was a list of things to try in order to reconnect. I highly doubted any of them would work. I barely heard Jeanie talking until she took her turn swearing: "Oh God. This is the absolute last fucking thing we need."

She had checked her connection and found the same thing I had: a screen letting us know how utterly disconnected we both were.

"Maybe it'll come back," I said. I didn't believe it though. I believed things would only continue to get worse. I turned out to be right on that count.

We bantered a bit more. It was uncomfortable, as was the world. Somehow, we left the conversation feeling a bit better. I'm confident stating that on her behalf because I heard it in her voice. I heard relief, I heard appreciation for a human connection, and I felt the same. We reassured each other that everything would be fine soon, as people do in situations where it looks like things will never be fine again. She told me that Eunice would be up and running again in no time. I told her that her daughters would likely be doing the same, maybe even chasing Eunice through the nearby trails.

I got another laugh out of her by the time we got off the phone. I appreciated that laugh, especially now as I look back on things and how they all unfolded. I treasure that sound, and always will. Because the next time I heard Jeanie Morneau's voice, it was because she was screaming.

After I got off the phone with Jeanie, I made a few other phone calls. I tried Derby Reynolds, my editor and friend, again. I had last spoken to him on the day of Eunice's run. That hadn't even been a week ago, but it felt like another lifetime. In that other lifetime, getting his feedback on my latest Freddy the Fearless Feline book had often been the highlight of my day. That felt absurd now given all we were facing.

I was dismayed but unsurprised when his phone went straight to voicemail. I left him a message for the third time since the last time I'd spoken to him via email. When he had told me that he was heading to the hospital because of an allergic reaction (a skin rash and irritated eyes), I hadn't thought much of it other than to hope and expect that he would get well soon. With all that had happened since, I had to wonder if he would ever get well, and if I would ever hear from him again. I did my best to push that extreme thought from my mind.

I once again wished Derby a speedy recovery, as I had the last two times I'd left a message, though this time it truly was a wish. It was a prayer I hoped would be answered. For him, for Eunice, for Jeanie's two little girls, and everyone afflicted. Even Ben and his wife.

Next, I called my cousin Heather Haynes in Toronto, Canada. I was nearly over the moon to get a response. I quickly fell back to Earth when she told me what was going on up there.

The news there wasn't good. Her twelve-year-old son, Brady, had been at a sleepover when the lockdown was called. He had gone to visit a friend on Sunday afternoon, not intending to stay there. With the extreme winds that had picked up as the day progressed, his friend's parents had offered to have Brady sleep over rather than risk the weather on his return home. Now, Heather wasn't even allowed to go and get her son, and was currently quarantining with her husband. Both of them were worried out of their minds about Brady, and angry at the government for keeping them separated.

Heather told me all she knew, which wasn't any more than what I knew. Her internet had cut out that morning as well. She and her husband were going stir crazy, and just a little bit crazy in general. I could tell she would have cried had we stayed on the line any longer than we had. I didn't blame her. I might have joined her.

We said a heartfelt goodbye, telling each other that we loved each other for the first time since we were children. I hoped it wouldn't be the last time, though I feared that it might be.

I got off the phone wishing I had found out how things were going there in more detail. I wanted to know what was going on in India as well, where the first black dandelion had been spotted and reported. I wanted to know what was going on in Seattle, where Derby was likely quarantined in the hospital (I hoped). But I couldn't find anything out; the internet was down.

After attempting to refresh it for hours and going through the process of troubleshooting to find out what the problem might be, I was certain it would continue to stay down. Calling my service provider had been no help. There hadn't been an answer. I imagine they were slammed with calls from people desperate to know what had gone wrong with their connection.

I called Eunice's sister in Arizona. She was quarantined with her husband in their condo. Both were healthy, both were worried about Eunice, and neither had the answers I was hoping to find. Their internet had been cut as well.

I called plenty of others: friends, family members, colleagues, and even fans I had met while promoting my books on social media. After all of those calls, I learned nothing other than the fact that worry doesn't have a cap on it. A person can gain worries exponentially, without limit. I was living proof of that. Because, as much as I had increased my worries after making those phone calls, I knew there were still many concerns to be added.

Eunice woke up at around two in the afternoon. "Baby?" she called out. It was the strongest she had sounded since our failed effort to go to the hospital. I began to go over to the room, feeling as optimistic as I could remember feeling since this whole ordeal had begun. Then she said: "Mort? Are you angry with me again? Please answer me." Mort. Her ex-husband.

"Are you okay, Eunice? It's me, Alex. Not Mort. I'm coming into the room... I don't want you to be scared, okay?"

"Alex?" She sounded genuinely baffled. Hearing the confusion in her voice broke my heart. I had read that rubella could progress in such a way that causes inflammation of the brain, seizures, and brain damage. The idea of having to watch Eunice as her brain deteriorated made me nearly break down right then. I pushed on instead, settling my chair in the doorway.

"Alex... My eyes, I think they've gotten even worse. They feel funny," she said from the bed. I didn't like the sound of that, but I was relieved that she had said my name with more certainty this time. She sounded like herself again, no longer confused. Though I almost wished she had been confused about what she was saying in this instance. I couldn't have imagined her eyes getting worse. However, I didn't have to imagine it, I could see it for myself. Even in the dim light of the bedroom, I could see how terrible things had gotten.

I looked at her, took a short sharp breath and held it, not knowing what to say or do. There was the urge to cry again. An urge that I fought. I couldn't allow myself to pity her. She wouldn't accept it. She had never pitied me in those early years when all I did was pity myself. But it was hard not to feel sorrow seeing the condition she was in.

The infection had worsened. What had looked like a mossy green film over her eyes before now looked like a thick layer of lichen had grown from beneath her eyelids and had spread and settled on top of them, fully encasing them like a set of thick green glasses. That wasn't the most distressing part, though. The worst part of what was emerging from her eyes wasn't the green growth, it was the little buds that had started to sprout out of that growth like flowers in a small field.

They were black, and though they hadn't fully developed yet, I knew they were the beginnings of tiny dandelions. Black dandelions were growing out of my wife's eyes.

I wanted to throw up, I wanted to turn and roll away and hyperventilate somewhere she wouldn't hear me. Instead, I said: "There's good news, babe. They think what you have is an advanced case of rubella. They're already working on a vaccine that should be here soon. And they're going to tweak it and do all that science-y stuff I don't understand until they get something that'll fix you up. Hopefully soon as well."

The last part of that statement wasn't quite true. I hadn't heard anything about a cure being anywhere close, but I knew they were working on one. I was trying to be optimistic again. More importantly, I was trying to spread that optimism to Eunice. A rare reversal of roles for us.

"You think we could go outside for a little? For a walk?" she responded. It was as if she hadn't heard anything I'd said about rubella or a potential vaccine and cure. Maybe she didn't believe it. I barely believed it myself. But it didn't matter, the actual positive news was that she felt strong enough to want to go for a walk. I wondered how long it would be before she was insisting she could run again, blind or not, bullheaded as she was.

The idea of her running again lifted my spirits ever so slightly. She hadn't even hinted at wanting to leave the bed since we had returned from trying to get to the hospital with the drone chasing behind us. I wanted to say yes, nothing would be better than going for a stroll with my wife, but there was one thing all of the news sites I had seen on the internet agreed on, whether they were mainstream or conspiratorial: everyone should stay indoors, especially those already infected; symptoms could dramatically worsen otherwise. "Sorry, Eunice," I said morosely. "Not yet. Not until you get better."

Until this point, she had been on her side, facing me. When I declined her request to go outdoors, she rolled onto her back, facing the ceiling. My stomach roiled after she did this. I could more distinctly see the little flower buds protruding from the green growth covering her eyes. I hoped my own eyes were playing tricks on me, because it looked like the buds were quivering and twitching and shifting around. I had to close my eyes for a moment, only opening them when she spoke again: "Alex? Could you get me some water, please? With sugar in it. And honey too."

I told her I would be back right away. I have never maneuvered my chair as quickly as I did then. I spun and headed toward the kitchen. By the time I got there, I did the bit of hyperventilating that I had held off on before. After catching my breath and trying to come to terms with what I had just seen, I did as Eunice had asked; I got her the sweetened water she'd requested. The entire while I could only think one thing: Whatever it is that's going around, it has nothing to do with rubella.

The internet never did return, and because everything we watched was streamed, I couldn't access the local news either. There were no emergency alerts on my cellphone to tell me what I could expect over the coming days. I had never felt so lost.

Not long after leaving Eunice in the bedroom and returning to the couch in the den, I began thinking of how I might ration out the food we had in the house. I was glad we had ordered a ton of groceries over the weekend. I wondered when, if ever, I'd be able to make another grocery order. It was a devastating thought, really contemplating that you might be cut off from society. Maybe permanently.

I told myself that I was getting ahead of myself, but it didn't feel that way. I was aware that my wife was in the house with me, but I felt entirely alone. I was reminded that I wasn't alone, however, every time Ben from across the road would step onto his balcony and scream out to the group of houses on our street. I didn't need the internet to bone up on my conspiracy theories with Ben right there shouting every bit of lunacy he could think of as he paced his balcony. Part of his most recent rant: "IT'S ALL AN EXPERIMENT! THEY'VE GODDAMNED POISONED US ALL AND THEY WANT TO SEE WHAT HAPPENS! CHEMICAL WARFARE IS WHAT THIS IS! WE'RE UNDER ATTACK FROM RED CHINA! WE'VE GONE TO WAR WITH THOSE GODDAMN SAVAGES AND NO ONE WANTS TO ADMIT WE'VE LOST!"

Sometimes he said it was Russia we were at war with (those "Ruskies," as he called them). Sometimes he claimed the United States government had sold its citizens to the highest bidder to be experimented on. I think he may have mentioned something breaking loose from Area 51 and causing all of this. My favorite was his theory on the black dandelions being the result of alien sperm sprayed all over the planet from above. He didn't say a word about rubella.

Odd as it sounds, I was relieved to hear someone else's voice, even if it was Ben's, and even though he was slowly going crazier by the day. I figured Jeanie must have felt the same on some level, because I never heard her call out to him to be silent either.

I constantly wondered what might be happening to Josh at any given moment. The kid was a brat, but I still thought he was decent at his core. Regardless, I didn't think he or his friends deserved what had happened to them. Or what might be happening to them if the conspiracy theories on experimentation were even partially true. I stopped myself from thinking those thoughts. Convinced myself that Josh and his friends were being held and quarantined safely somewhere for their own good and for the good of the rest of society since Josh had failed to follow the rules.

From time to time throughout the day I would go to the window and look at his home, thinking maybe he had been returned at some point and I'd missed it. But that was wishful thinking. There was no sign of life in his house.

I had his parents' cell phone numbers, and considered giving them a call, but I didn't have the heart to tell them what had happened. If I'd had any answers, I might have called and given them the news. However, by the time evening rolled around, it didn't matter whether or not I wanted to call them. I wouldn't have been able to.

After the internet had cut out, I'd been able to make several calls. Even if I hadn't been able to reach the people I'd called, I was still able to connect to their lines, get the ringing sound and the voicemail system.

But at around 5:00 PM on May 4, 2045, when I decided to call my editor and friend, Derby, one more time, I got nothing.

I looked at the screen of my phone, thinking maybe I hadn't hit dial, but that wasn't the case. The call simply wouldn't connect. I tried again and got the same thing.

I called my cousin, Heather, in Canada and this time got a busy signal. Even as I desperately attempted to make about two dozen more phone calls, I knew I was wasting my time. And I think I knew what was happening.

I'm pretty sure the cell towers were overloaded. People who hadn't made a call in decades were now all running to their phones to use them as actual phones for the first time in years. The cell towers likely couldn't handle the influx of calls. At least I hoped that was all it was. Ben, however, had other theories.

Not long after I gave up on trying to call my friends and family, Ben, from his balcony, provided another explanation: THEY'RE CUTTING US OFF FROM OUR LOVED ONES! IT'S ONLY A MATTER OF TIME BEFORE THEY KILL US ALL! IT'LL BE BOMBS, I BET! WHEN THEY'RE TIRED OF THIS EXPERIMENT, IT'LL BE BOMBS!"

I'm not sure how long Ben stayed out there on his balcony yelling that evening. After a few minutes of listening to his shrill voice, I turned on some music. Fortunately, I had a small library of songs downloaded to my laptop that I didn't have to stream.

Mostly songs from the mid to late 2010s when I'd been an angsty teenager. I put the songs on just loud enough to block out Ben, but not loud enough to disturb Eunice.

I let my wife sleep until I had no choice but to disturb her. I had to give her the antibiotics that I was quickly realizing weren't going to help anyone in this situation. I took the medication to her anyway, along with a gloopy part-water, part-sugar, part-honey mixture in a half-gallon jug. I also brought her two bottles of sugar water. It was all she would take in.

We had run out of orange juice the previous day. I had planned to order more today, though with the internet down... I tried not to think about what it might mean for us if the net didn't come back up. Usually, I would be comforted by the fact that I could call somewhere and ask for what I needed, but with the phonelines jammed we might have to survive off of whatever supplies we had stored in the house for a while; supplies which were quickly dwindling.

In the last few days, Eunice had gone through nearly a pound of a two-pound bag of sugar, and our honey was running low. There was maple syrup after that, then we would have to see how Eunice would fare without anything sugary to put into her system. My hope was that she would be recovered by then. My hope was severely diminished when I remembered what was growing out of her eyes.

I had barely entered the bedroom before Eunice said: "Alex? Are you sure we can't go outside?"

"Not for a little while, babe. Not until you get better. Right now, outside is bad for you." I had said this several times that day. She seemed to forget each time. Or maybe she just wanted me to change my answer. Eunice always had been stubborn.

She asked for water again. I rolled the cart I had pushed ahead of me until it was beside her. I watched her sit up and slowly grope her way over the items on top of the cart until she found the antibiotic pill and the jug of water. They were both consumed quickly. I watched her hands as she found the bottles of water on the tray as well. She quickly chugged those too. I watched her hands because I couldn't bring myself to look her in the face. Not when those black buds were protruding from her eyes. The rash on her face and hands wasn't clearing up either.

Eunice was wearing a sweatshirt and sweatpants. She hadn't showered or changed out of those clothes since going to bed on Sunday after her run. I considered asking her to do that now. Not only because the smell coming from her was overpowering, but to see if the rash had spread to the areas underneath her clothes. I decided not to bother; it would be a lot to ask of her given her condition.

While she seemed stronger than she had been the day before, she was still more fragile than I had ever seen her. I decided the shower and change of clothes could wait. Besides, if the rash had spread, there was nothing I could do about it. All I could do was hope for the meds to work, for the internet to come back, and for the authorities to have a solution. That wasn't too much to ask, right? As it turned out, it was too much to ask, but I didn't know that then.

"We can't go outside, but what if we go on a different kind of adventure? If you're up for it, of course," I said to her. I was trying to sound as positive as possible, looking everywhere but at her face, and feeling relieved she couldn't see how disturbed and uncomfortable I was by the sight of her. She asked: "What do you mean?"

The question was a little slow and slurred, but it meant she understood what I had asked enough to want me to elaborate. I took that as a good sign. I was looking for good signs wherever I could find them.

"I'm going to read to you for a bit, if you're up for it. The internet's down and I was going to do some reading in the den. I figured we might as well enjoy a story together."

"Sounds... nice. Read loud, please. You sound... far."

That was definitely not a good sign. I swallowed the lump in my throat and continued to try to sound both louder and more cheerful when I told her: "I dug up your favorite book from the library. Slaughterhouse-Five."

I looked at her face then, because I had to see her reaction to know that she was still herself. What I saw made me want to cry then and there. Her face was partially covered with a mahogany-colored rash, her eyes were grown over by something I couldn't explain or get rid of. The parts of her face that weren't covered by the rash were ashen. Eunice had always been pale, but now she looked nearly translucent.

Even with everything wrong with her at the moment, she looked beautiful to me because she smiled. She always smiled at the mention of Slaughterhouse-Five by Kurt Vonnegut. In that moment, her smile made her seem more herself than she had been since before all of this began.

I sat by the doorway and read the story, loudly and clearly, from beginning to end. It took nearly seven hours, including several breaks for sugar water (and bathroom breaks for me, but none for her), along with a few interruptions from Ben, who went back and forth from his usual rants to yelling at or for his wife. I didn't envy Gloria for having to share a house with that man even in the best of times. I tuned him out and focused on reading to Eunice.

As I read, she would sometimes ask me to repeat myself. I worried she wasn't understanding, but she was with me the entire while. She was listening, she comprehended, and she was with me.

I had always enjoyed the story, but I never loved it as much as she did, possibly because I didn't quite understand it. But it clicked with me this time. It meant much more given our circumstances, and how little hope there seemed to be.

At the end of the story, she thanked me and smiled again. Then, judging by the change in her breathing, she fell asleep. It was an odd response that left me uncertain how to feel. She always cried at the end of Slaughterhouse-Five; she had told me that several times. I had seen it once for myself. Yet, at that moment, she slept with a small smile on her face.

So it goes, I thought to myself as I looked at her sleeping face and all the things on it that I couldn't explain. With her eyes completely grown over, I wondered if she *could* cry. I suppose it didn't matter. At that moment, I was crying enough for both of us.

Friday, May 5, 2045

A scream woke me up. I had slept in the hallway outside of our bedroom the entire night with Slaughterhouse-Five on my lap. The scream jolted me enough to make me drop the book. I was too concerned with what I had just heard to pick it up.

I looked in on my wife to see if either the scream or the sound of the book dropping had woken her up. Neither had. I headed for the den window and the sound that had woken me.

"DAISY! ROSE! STAY INSIDE! DON'T GO OUT THERE!

It was Jeanie. She hadn't been kidding when she'd said her girls were getting their strength back. Like Eunice, they must have been eager to get back outdoors. It was enough for me to feel optimistic, if only slightly. I pictured the little kids running around the house giving their mother heck. It would have put a smile on my face except for the second scream that came from Jeanie. This time it sounded like she was in pain. Following that, she cried for them to "STOP!" and "COME BACK!" Then she screamed "NO!" several times. This wasn't just a mother wanting her kids to avoid the outdoors, something was seriously wrong.

By that time, I was at the window. I pried the blinds apart and looked over at Jeanie's house. Her front door and windows were closed, but I could still hear her clearly, which shouldn't have been the case if she was inside the house. It sounded like the cries were coming from the backyard. She and her kids often played back there.

After the dustup with her husband, she had invited the neighborhood for a barbeque. A "Get to know me before you label me as a gun toting train wreck" sort of affair. We had all enjoyed the solarium that Ben had nearly stopped from being created. The kids practically had an entire park to themselves back there. It made sense that they would head to the backyard after getting their strength back. However, there was the warning about staying indoors to worry about.

The authorities had repeated several times that it was of the utmost importance for those infected to avoid the sun and the outdoors in general. They hadn't specified any details, only stated that it would make the symptoms of this illness worse. Ben had been ignoring that advice with his periodic rants from his balcony, and he seemed to be deteriorating (at least mentally) at a rapid rate.

With that in mind, I understood why Jeanie was screaming frantically for her kids to stay inside. I watched intently, waiting for movement or some sound, anything that might let me know what to do. I wanted to go over there but didn't feel as though I should. Maybe I could be considered a coward because of that, but I didn't want to abandon my wife. And if I caught what was going around, I would be useless to us both.

I felt helpless. Though when I considered calling for help, I wondered if the police would have time to come out here with all of the chaos likely going on in the city. I wondered if the call would even go through if I made it, considering the cell towers were jammed the way they were. I wondered, most strongly, if what had happened to Josh and his friends might happen to Jeanie and her kids if I called the police there. I didn't want to risk it, but after listening to her scream, did I really have a choice?

Getting my phone, I pressed 9 and 1. Once again, my finger didn't immediately press the final 1. Not until I heard Jeanie begin to scream again. This time it was the names of her daughters: "Daisy! Rose!" repeated time and time again with no context between. She was simply shrieking their names, until, after a while, she was just shrieking.

I pressed the final digit. Right after I did, the cries diminished until I could no longer hear Jeanie from across the street at all.

I didn't think I could be more afraid during this ordeal than I already had been, but there I was with my heart in my ears, my mouth dry, and my head full of dark thoughts about what might be going on with my friend and neighbor's two little girls. I put the phone to my face with a trembling hand.

With my left ear I was relieved to find that I could actually hear a ringtone. Perhaps only emergency calls could go through. I waited impatiently for the operator to answer. With my right ear I strained to hear anything going on from the house across the street.

In my left ear I heard the words: "9-1-1. What's your emergency?" from a female operator who sounded as stressed as I felt. In my right ear was the silence of the neighborhood. It carried a weight I could nearly feel pressing down on me.

"It's my neighbor. Across the street from me. There was screaming. Her daughters were sick and she was screaming and now she's not screaming and I'm not sure what's happening," I said to the person on the line, realizing I sounded far more frantic than I wanted to, though likely less so than I felt. I desperately wanted to hear something from Jeanie's house to know that she was okay.

"I'll need you to please try and stay calm, sir. Is there an actual emergency that you can identify other than screaming? We're rammed with calls at the moment. Can you give me any more information about what is going on?"

I was going to say that I couldn't. Then that changed. In a split second, that changed entirely. Because there was a sound that gave me at least something solid to tell the operator. It was a single sound booming into the air before quickly going back to silence. It was a sound and silence I will never forget. I said to the emergency dispatch operator: "Oh my God, there's been a gunshot! I think someone might have been shot!"

I gave her Jeanie's name and address. I don't remember much else of the brief interaction. I only remember clutching my phone in one hand as I parted the blinds with the other. My heart thudded in a way that made it feel like it might pop at any second as I stared at Jeanie's house. I was waiting anxiously for another sound. Something that would come before the sirens. Anything that would let me know Jeanie and her girls were okay.

The sound of the sirens never came, neither did any sound from Jeanie's house. I saw two vehicles pull up in front of her house not long after I had placed the call to the police. If I hadn't been watching from the window, I might have missed the response vehicles altogether.

There was a black SUV and a yellow hazardous transport ambulance identical to the one that had pulled onto the street and left with Josh and his house guests the other night. I hoped this wouldn't turn out the way that had. Of course, that was a foolish hope. Or at least it seemed to be as I watched two armed and HAZMAT-suited people approach Jeanie's house, giving me flashbacks to what had happened to Josh.

They crept toward the door with their weapons ready as a SWAT team would, knocking first, then announcing themselves before the lead officer opened the door. Jeanie had apparently not bothered to lock it. She likely wasn't expecting either visitors or intruders while this contagion was going around.

I was a living, breathing bundle of nerves as the officers entered Jeanie's house. I don't know how much time actually passed between when they went in and when they came out, but it seemed like a week had gone by before they emerged empty handed. Their weapons were no longer up and ready to fire. They must have determined there was no issue in the household. That was confirmed to me when they walked to the yellow ambulance and signalled to the people inside of it.

I thought that might be a positive thing. However, moments later, a gurney was slowly rolled out of the back of the emergency vehicle, causing my nerves to be further set on fire. Someone was hurt... at least hurt... and the emergency service personnel didn't seem to be in a rush to aid them. That was never a good sign.

Along with the gurney, two HAZMAT-suited people who I presumed to be paramedics left the ambulance and entered the house. The two who had entered first returned to the black SUV. The wait for the paramedics to return from the house was unbearable, and the end of that wait was even worse.

The paramedics came out of the house with a body on the gurney. To my dismay, that body was inside of a body bag, confirming my suspicions about why the officers and paramedics had reacted almost nonchalantly after Jeanie's home had been searched. There was no one to save in that household, only people to collect.

I was shaking, my lungs hurt because I had been holding my breath for so long. I kept looking at the body bag, knowing Jeanie was in it based on its size and shape. I was hoping she would sit up, let herself out, and let the medics know they had made a huge mistake. But that didn't happen. The body in the bag was loaded into the back of the hazardous transport vehicle. They closed the doors. I closed my eyes momentarily and prayed that the next two bodies that emerged from the house would do so on their own feet. I prayed that Jeanie's little girls were okay.

When I opened my eyes, I expected the medics to be heading back into the house to bring out the two children, but after shutting the back of the ambulance, the medics returned to their spots in the cab of the vehicle. I was horrified to see that both vehicles seemed to be preparing to go.

It was then that I did something I hadn't thought through. I pulled up the blinds, opened the window and yelled out to the emergency response team: "Hey! What about the kids? What about the two little girls? And my wife! My wife is sick in here! She's not doing well! Please, don't leave us like this!"

They didn't hear me, or they pretended not to hear me. Maybe they just didn't care. The vehicles were driving around the little roundabout in the middle of the cul-de-sac and were exiting with the SUV in the lead as I was still shouting for them to come back and help us. By then my voice was drowned out by the wind, their engines, and by the yelling of someone else. Ben had emerged on his balcony, and he was shouting at the vehicles too.

"Please! Whoever is out there! Can you help? HELP US! My wife! She's gone! She went out to the backyard, and she never came back! I can't see, and I can't find her! PLEASE!"

It was then I recalled that Ben had been yelling for Gloria the day before as I read to Eunice, ignoring what I hadn't realized were attempts to find his missing wife. I felt guilty for ignoring him but understood there was nothing I could have done. Apparently, the emergency response team felt the same because they were driving away. His cries were as futile as mine. Whether or not they could hear us, they wouldn't turn around. That didn't stop Ben from screaming even louder: "SOMEONE HELP! ANYONE! HELP! PLEASE DON'T LEAVE US! MY WIFE! I CAN'T SEE!

"They're gone, Ben!" I called out from behind the mesh screen of my open window, feeling foolish for letting the outside air in. "Try to go inside and drink water and rest! They'll be back when they have this thing figured out!"

I said this in an attempt to convince myself of it as much as I was trying to convince him. I hadn't expected him to hear me, let alone listen to me, but he stopped his shouting. He looked at me from his balcony. At least it seemed as though he did, but I knew he couldn't see me. Even though his face was aimed in the direction of my house, he couldn't see me because the moss had grown over his eyes much as it had grown over Eunice's. Though it didn't seem as if his moss had... bloomed yet. I'm not sure what else to call it, but his eyes weren't sprouting the tiny black buds Eunice's were. At least not that I could tell from this distance. I thought that might be a positive thing. Then I remembered the world I was currently in, and remembered that just about everything was negative. His next actions confirmed this. I barely had time to react before he did it.

I think my exact words were: "BEN! NO!" But by then he was already climbing the railing of the balcony. There hadn't been any emotion on his face as he did it. It seemed like a task that just had to be done.

I'll never forget that look. What's worse, I'll never forget the sound Ben's skull made as he landed following the twenty-foot drop from his balcony to the flagstone walkway below. It reminded me of the crack of a baseball bat when someone has hit a pitch squarely; a no-doubter out of the park. That's what the sound reminded me of.

He landed directly on his head. It burst. That's how I see it in my memory. His head simply... burst.

His head hit the stone and broke open. His body folded over onto itself in a way that seemed impossible. His neck broke. I saw it and heard it. It was mixed in with the cracking sound of Ben's skull, but it resonated slightly differently; the first sound was a crack, the second a crunch. The next noise after that was my voice calling out to Ben. I don't know why I kept calling to him, he was dead. That was beyond any doubt. In a way, that might have been true even before he had jumped.

I called 9-1-1 again. I was still by the window but now it was closed. I couldn't bear to look out between the blinds. I didn't want to see Ben's body laying there on his walkway. It took me a few tries to get a ringtone again. When I did, the phone rang for quite a while before someone answered. It was a male operator this time. One who sounded on edge as he said: "9-1-1. What's your emergency?"

The last time I had been frantic; this time I was calm, or at least I tried my best to be. Eunice had slept through everything. I didn't want to wake her now. I told the operator about Ben, and the way he was dead on his property.

"Did you say your neighbor is dead, sir? Were you able to check his vitals?"

"I... He was infected before he died. As far as I can tell, I'm not infected yet. I don't want to risk going outside. But his head is damaged very badly, and his neck is broken. He hasn't moved since he fell. I'm sure he's gone."

My calm was breaking as I talked about it. Talking about it made it real. I might have cried then, for the second time since this whole nightmare began, except what the operator said next switched my emotion from sadness to anger. "There's nothing we can do about that, sir. Not immediately anyway. I'll put in a note, and when things normalize a bit we will send someone there to collect the body."

"That *body* is my neighbor! What do you mean nothing can be done? You can't just leave him rotting in the street."

I heard the operator take a deep breath. He was trying to maintain his composure as I was losing mine. I heard him exhale before speaking, his voice sounded like he might be on the verge of tears of his own. "Sir. I'm getting calls about things that don't even make sense to me. There are emergencies all over the county right now. Unfortunately, a dead body isn't one of them. Believe me, I wish it was. Do us all a favor: stay away from your neighbor's body. And stay indoors."

I sat there, shocked. I couldn't believe what I was hearing. I was angry and indignant. Though by the time I was ready to respond, I realized he had disconnected the call.

The next thing I did after being hung up on by the 9-1-1 dispatcher was make a difficult decision. First, I checked on Eunice, thankful she had stayed asleep through everything I'd heard and witnessed. Then, I grabbed my raincoat.

I knew I shouldn't go outside. I was certain I shouldn't cross the road and enter my neighbor's house, but I had to. And not for Ben's sake. God rest him, he was one hundred percent dead. And, according to him, his wife had run off somewhere. I could barely blame her with the way he had been behaving during this whole thing. As bad as that makes me feel to think and write down, it was the truth. The reason I needed to risk being in the midst of whatever was out there in the air, was because there were two little girls unaccounted for who might still be in or around Jeanie Morneau's house. I knew I would never sleep again if I didn't go see what had happened to them myself.

Covering up completely, I said another small prayer, then I went across the street to find Jeanie's daughters.

I couldn't go through the front door of Jeanie's house with my chair because of the steps leading up to it. Thankfully, the slope of the lawn was gentle, and because it hadn't rained in nearly a week, the grass was firm. I had no trouble gaining traction. My main concern was the fact that I was rolling over a lawn full of black dandelions, collecting a combination of crushed black petals and fluffy white seeds on my wheels. I had to touch those wheels with my hands because maneuvering along terrain like this was easier to do manually than with the electronic function of the chair, which I rarely used in any case.

I had nitrile gloves on beneath a pair of faux leather gloves. I was too paranoid to make contact with the crushed black dandelions. I was determined not to be directly touched by anything outside of my home.

I was able to go around the house to the backyard, fortunate that the gate had been left wide open. I would have been able to get it open regardless, but that would have meant more time sitting in the black dandelion filled grass.

The scene in the backyard wasn't what I'd expected. To be fair, I don't know what I'd expected. Maybe two small bodies laying dead in the grass, I suppose. That was what was on my mind when I entered the yard, moving along the stone path from the gate to the deck and the solarium attached to Jeanie's house. The deck and the backyard were covered in dandelion fluff. The entire yard was white.

Even before I got to the house I could tell what had happened to Jeanie; what she had done. Through the glass of the solarium, I could see an overturned patio chair. Behind it, on the ground and on the back wall, there was a red stripe, like someone had lazily spray-painted part of Jeanie's property. I wish spray paint was all it was. Directly behind and beneath the overturned chair was what I was sure was a pool of blood. I looked for the gun I had heard, but couldn't see it. Like Jeanie's body, it had most likely been removed by the authorities.

I was no blood spatter analyst or detective, but it didn't take a professional to figure out that the blood I was seeing was from Jeanie Morneau. I didn't want to picture it, but I couldn't stop the image of her sitting in that chair, putting a gun to her head, and pulling the trigger from running through my mind. But why? Where were her kids?

The backyard was fenced in. The fences were six feet high. Behind them was a dense stretch of wooded area which the trails Eunice had so regularly run along cut through. Could the girls have climbed the fence and wandered into that bit of wood? At three and five years old, I couldn't imagine it. If they'd gone through the gate I'd entered, I would have seen them when I'd been looking at the house as Jeanie had screamed for them to come back inside.

I called out for both Daisy and Rose. I approached the solarium and the open back door and shouted into the house, getting no response from either of them. It struck me then that every house in the neighborhood was now empty except for mine. I can't recall ever having a lonelier thought.

I looked around the backyard again. Other than the white fluff, the black dandelions, and a pair of exotic new shrubs I couldn't identify which had likely been planted since the last time Eunice and I had been back here for a visit, I saw nothing out of the ordinary.

I considered getting out of my chair and crawling into the solarium and through the house. Only a couple of steps prevented me from doing so. But I considered how Jeanie had screamed for her children before the gunshot, and what Ben had said before he had plunged to his death. I knew that neither of my neighbors would have acted as they had if their loved ones hadn't been gone without a doubt.

Two children and a middle-aged woman had just vanished, all three of them infected by whatever contagion was going around.

I decided against crawling around the house, not only because I was sure I wouldn't find anything, but because thinking of Jeanie's and Ben's infected loved ones made me think of my own. Eunice, who had been begging to go outside for days, and who was now alone with no one to stop her. I thought of her in a panic as I wondered about the vanished family members of my neighbors. I couldn't help but worry she might be next.

With that thought consuming my mind, I turned and headed back for home and to my wife as quickly as I could.

The smell hit me as soon as I opened the door to my house. A smell of dirt and freshly cut grass. It was stronger than ever. I must have gone nose blind to it while cooped up in there with Eunice. After leaving and returning, the smell was like an uppercut to my nose even through my mask. It only grew stronger as I got closer to the bedroom. As always, the bedroom door was wide open. The open door allowed me to see the bed. The bed that should have been occupied by Eunice but was empty.

In that moment I could almost hear Ben screaming what were among his final words: "My Wife! She's gone!" from the balcony before he jumped. Could I blame him? In the middle of what I was beginning to think of as an apocalyptic event, his partner had vanished on him while his failing vision meant the rest of the world had vanished as well. Even though I could still see, I knew that everything would be dimmed without Eunice in my life. The world would be dark even at midday; she was my life and my light. I needed her at that moment more than ever. But her bed was empty. I was terrified she was gone.

I rolled into the bedroom. It too was empty. My heart was in my throat, stopping me from breathing. I hadn't had a full-blown panic attack in years, but I felt one coming on. Then I heard a noise from the bathroom that helped to put me at ease.

The shower was running. That was a positive, I thought. It had to be a positive, because she had barely been able to move a few days ago. Now she was strong enough to get up and take a shower. I told myself it had to be a good thing. However, I still had a heavy feeling in my chest. I would like to say that it was a feeling that something wasn't right, but nothing was right at the moment. It was more of a feeling that nothing would ever be right again.

I turned toward the bathroom. I was going to go to it, to knock and ask how she was doing, just as the door opened. On the other side of the threshold between our room and the bathroom was the confirmation of my bad feeling. Eunice was not doing well.

She had been in the shower with her clothes on. She was drenched and dripping water all over the floor as she entered the bedroom. She walked without seeing, but somehow didn't seem to be struggling with her lack of sight. She walked into the bedroom without stumbling or hesitating. She seemed strong and steady, but I couldn't take that to be a sign of improvement because I could see that she had lost her hair at some point overnight.

Most of her long, beautiful hair had fallen right out, leaving a few black tufts here and there around the crown of her skull. Her skin was almost unrecognizable. Despite the fact that she had been indoors for nearly a week, parts of her looked as though she had been left out in the sun to burn, then to crispen. The skin of her face and hands, where the rash had been, had turned a baffling shade of brown and had become wrinkled. Eunice looked like she had aged nearly fifty years in the span of a night.

I want to say she appeared to be dazed, but it's hard to determine what a person's mental state might be when you can't see what they're looking at. Her eyes were overgrown by what now clearly looked like lichen, and the little black flower buds which had grown there the day before were in full bloom. They shook with each step she took. Those black dandelions were the only thing about her that wavered. Her jaw, which was covered with wrinkled and discolored skin, looked set; she faced me straight on as if looking directly at me. I couldn't stop staring at the flowers protruding from her eyes. My stomach churned as I watched them wobbling in her head.

The situation was incomprehensible. How could this have happened? How did we all wind up like this? Those were the questions running through my head as I reversed my chair, backing my way toward the door as Eunice kept marching forward. It was then that she spoke, sending a chill running through my body. Very calmly, she said: "I need to go outside."

Hearing her speak woke me from a daze I hadn't even realized I was in. I had put myself directly before the bedroom door. I was blocking her way toward the hall and the path to the front entry, wanting to stop her at all costs from winding up like the loved ones of my neighbors. Somehow, despite not being able to see me there, I think she knew my intentions were to not allow her to leave.

"We have to stay inside, Eunice. You especially. That's what the experts are saying." I didn't think she cared much about what the experts were saying, but I felt like I had to say that to validate my trying to stop her. She only repeated herself in a cold voice that didn't sound much like her at all: "I have to go outside."

"No, baby, you don't. You have to stay here and get better," was my reply. She stopped in front of me. For a split second, I thought maybe I'd gotten through to her. I saw that she was looking at me through her flower-clotted eyes. I became certain that she could somehow see me despite the bacteria (whatever this was) growing out of her eyes. "I have to go outside," she repeated. And I repeated that she couldn't.

It was the only time in our nearly twenty-five years together that I had ever told her that she couldn't do something she intended to do. It was most definitely the first time I had tried to block her physically from doing what she wanted. But I was determined not to let her pass. All I knew was that two of my neighbors were dead, both having killed themselves after their loved ones had disappeared. Facing that realization in this moment, imagining myself in Ben and Jeanie's shoes, I understood why they had done what they had done. I just didn't want to have to do the same.

I put the brakes to my wheels on. I was set to be stationary right there in front of the door. I had no plans to let her pass. I said as much, telling her: "You can't go outside, Eunice. You have to stay here and get better."

In response to that, she reached down to my armrests and tipped my chair over.

I was as winded by my impact with the floor as I was by the fact that she had shoved me over. I felt betrayed for a moment, a flash of anger superseded the pain caused by my head crashing against the hardwood. Then I felt ashamed of myself for feeling that way toward her. She was sick with something that no one could explain. She wasn't herself. I kept telling myself that as I gathered myself on the ground. I pulled away from my seat, bore the discomfort of getting onto my stumps and balancing on them in order to tilt the chair upright. By then she was walking down the hallway and toward the front door.

"Eunice! Please don't!" I cried out to her, still struggling to get my chair upright. It wouldn't be the first time I had fallen out of my chair, though it was the first time I had been tipped out of it. I should have righted it faster, but I was shaking. I was terrified of what was happening to my wife, the only woman I had ever loved. I didn't know where she was going. I didn't know where she had gone. But I knew she wasn't all there. Part of her was. Part of her had to still be there because she responded to me for the last time. While walking down the hall, without turning, she said: "I have to go outside, Alex! I have to go!"

With that, she went. I managed to get myself back in my chair. I was able to turn around and head to the hallway. Eunice had already turned the corner and was making her way down the corridor that would take her to the front door. In my path, before I could turn the corner and follow her, was a small but distressing obstacle. It was the sweater she had been wearing. It was soaked and laying in a small puddle on the floor. A watery trail led to and from it. The hallway was wet where she had walked.

When I rolled over the sweater and around the corner, I saw her sweatpants in a similar condition. Then her underwear, followed by the shirt she had been wearing beneath her sweater. I looked up from the trail of clothes in my hallway and saw my naked wife opening the front door.

I called after her, I must have said her name a dozen times. She didn't respond at all. She didn't turn around or stop or answer. I watched her, feeling as useless as I can ever recall feeling. She walked into the morning sunshine as I tried to catch up, weaving around and rolling over the clothes she had removed and abandoned.

In the brightness of the outdoors, I could clearly see her body for the first time since the night before she had gone for her run. She was distressingly pale. Where her skin hadn't been exposed to the infection and turned wrinkled and brown, she was nearly as white as a cloud. Her skin was as translucent as wax paper. I could see beneath it. What I was looking at was a network of veins. They weren't the standard blue of veins showing through pale skin; her veins were a greenish brown, like sludge was running through her system.

The veins in her lower legs were especially distinct. They were as thick as fingers, and almost seemed to push and pulse against her skin as she walked. She was naked and sick and horrifying and beautiful and leaving me. I didn't know how to get her to return. Eunice was halfway across the lawn by the time I got to the front door and called out yet again for her to come back.

You won't be surprised when I tell you that not a single detail of that moment will ever leave my mind. It was disturbing beyond words. But yes, there was beauty in it too, as crazy as that sounds. It was a beginning as well as an end. This entire ordeal was.

My partner of nearly twenty-five years had gone to the edge of the lawn, not far from the street, stark naked as the day she had been born. The green-brown veins were apparent all over her, but they didn't strike me with the same revulsion they had when I'd first noticed them. Because, as I saw her stop on the lawn and turn her face toward the sky, I think I understood what was happening before her end came, and I understood it even better after.

My wife turned back in the direction of the house. For a fleeting moment I thought (desperately hoped) she would walk back to me, but she didn't. Instead, she fell to her knees as if in prayer. I suppose, in a sense, that's what this was.

She turned her head east, raised it to the sun. I would like to say she looked at the glowing disc burning bright in the sky, but her eyes were overgrown by flowers, and she couldn't see a thing.

She smiled nonetheless because she could feel it. And I suppose I could too. Change was coming. For her and for the world.

She raised her hands toward the sun as if physically feeling for its rays, her fingers opening and closing, summoning the sun's beams. After a few seconds, her fingers stopped moving. It was as if she was satisfied that they had received whatever it was that they had been reaching for. Her body stopped moving as well.

I watched in awe as the unaffected skin of my wife's body went from pale white to reddish brown, matching the color of what I had thought to be the rash on her face and hands. It didn't happen all at once; it was like a slow blush. It spread from her bosom (from her heart, is what I told myself when all was said and done) until it reached her unmoving hands, which were still raised toward the sun as if physically drawing energy from its rays.

Her red-brown skin hardened until I recognized it for what it was, and her for what she was becoming.

Watching her, I began to make sense of what had happened across the street: Ben's wife, Gloria, wandering blind into the backyard and going missing; Jeanie's two little girls, Rose and Daisy, running from their mother, going into their backyard never to be seen or heard from again, causing their mother to do what she had done. Except they *would* be seen again, though they would never be recognized for what they once had been. It would be the same for Eunice.

I nearly hesitate to write this down, because, even as I watched it, I didn't believe it. I couldn't believe it;

I didn't want to believe it. Until I had no choice but to. I couldn't deny it no matter how much I wanted to.

Eunice knelt in the grass among the black dandelions. Her lower legs had grown bright red as the veins there pulsated, pushed against her skin, then split it. Vein-like tendrils burst from the openings in Eunice's flesh. They spilled down her legs and into the ground like a horde of relentless worms, digging in and burrowing there.

I was crying by then, calling her name repeatedly, but knowing there was no point. I could only watch, fogging up my goggles until I eventually took them off. I didn't care anymore. As I watched what was happening to Eunice, I didn't think there was anything to care about any longer.

I looked at her face and saw that she was still smiling. I had never seen her look so serene and at peace the entire time I had known her. But that didn't make me feel any better, not in the moment. How could I feel anything but terror and pain when I was seeing something that should have been impossible?

With my goggles off and my vision clear, I saw that the tendrils that had ripped their way out of my wife's legs were roots, not veins. They were small roots, some of them continuing to worm their way out of her and into the ground all around her as a mass of them also crawled up her legs, covering her thighs, her hips, and winding themselves around her torso.

Looking at her skin, its color, and how it had wrinkled and appeared hardened, made me feel as though the sun was burning her at hyper speed. The skin of her torso was fusing with the roots spreading up from her legs. She was coarse all over, and had turned the color of mahogany. Except for where she was turning a different color.

At her arms, her shoulders, and her head, pink and white petals pushed their way out from inside of her, sprouting through what had once been her pores. Her face was fading away as the blossoms overtook her upper body.

The last thing I saw, before I could no longer quite recognize her beautiful features, was her smile. At least that's what I've convinced myself that I saw. It was brief, but I'm certain it was a smile. The smile only came to an end when she opened her mouth wide, creating a hollow in the small tree she had become.

I heard a coughing sound coming from what used to be my wife. It was loud and extended. From the hollow of her came a flurry of white. A spray of white like blown snow on a windy winter's day. Tiny particles, hundreds of thousands of them, like dandelion seeds, were spreading into the air. They changed the season momentarily, creating a blizzard in early May.

I sat there, weeping as I watched what my wife had become. I thought of the two unfamiliar shrubs I had seen in Jeanie Morneau's backyard. I thought of Ben and his missing wife. I thought of the end my two neighbors had faced, and I knew what I had to do next.

Without giving it a second thought, I removed my raincoat, I removed my mask, and I went over to sit beside my wife.

Sunday, May 7, 2045

I've spent the last two days completing this document. Going back, cleaning it up, and making sure everything is told as it happened, and in as much detail as I can remember. I've printed it out and left it on my desk, beneath the paperweight of my published Freddy the Fearless Feline books. I selfishly hope those books will still be beneficial to whatever society is left after this. If there is a society left at all.

To those who make it through this, if there is anyone who does make it through this, when you find this document and when you find my wife and I out there on the front lawn, I want you to understand what happened. Or at least what I believe happened. I want you to understand that there was a fight here, a battle we hadn't even known was going on.

It was a war we had started, and one that we were losing. It was a war against the world itself. Against Earth. One, I suppose, we had been winning for a while, if murder counts as victory. But when the black dandelions bloomed, that was Earth finally fighting back.

Forget the conspiracy theories and news reports that you read, the nonsense about the black dandelions being generated in a lab, or that they were a freak mutation. Or that this was God angry at man for sinning, smiting us because of it. Though I suppose that last theory is closer to the truth if you consider God to be nature and nature to be God. Because that was what this was: Man vs Nature. A war we declared hundreds of years ago against an unwitting enemy.

This was nature taking a stand after centuries of being mistreated, battered, and beaten. This was a war we began, unprovoked, and one we were not prepared for. Not at the end.

I originally titled this document "A Story of Survival" optimistically because I had hoped that Eunice and I would make it out of this alive, as we had the pandemic that had almost destroyed us nearly a quarter-century ago. When I realized that wouldn't be the case, I considered changing the title of this document. But as I looked at it, struggling to see as my eyesight began to fade, I realized the title was perfect.

I'm going to join my wife on the lawn now, perhaps for good this time. My vision is darkening and there is something out there calling to me; I like to think that it's her.

I just wanted to make sure that you understand the title of this document, this telling of what might be humanity's final days.

This *is* a story of survival, just not of ours.

THANKS FOR READING!

It's hard to talk about saving the environment without sounding preachy, so I won't elaborate on the points raised in Black Bloom. I'll only say that if the Earth could have revenge on humans for what we have done to it, it would be ugly. And we would deserve it.

But was Alexander Langston right? Were the black dandelions the result of the Earth seeking vengeance? Or was one of the conspiracy theories correct? Maybe Ben's assertion about alien sperm being dropped on the planet from above. I'll leave it up to you to decide. For now.

I thought of the idea for Black Bloom when I went for a run in May of 2021. It wasn't particularly windy from what I recall. But when I ran by a patch of dandelions that had turned white, the wind picked up and some of the dandelion fluff wound up in my eye. My imagination, being what it is, almost immediately caused me to picture dandelions growing out of my eyes as a result of this. By the end of the run, I had figured out the rudimentary plot of Black Bloom (originally titled "Spores").

I wanted to use this story as a way to explore the things that were on my mind at the time, namely the uncertainty of the future given all that was going on around the world: the pandemic, the recent protests and riots over police brutality, and, as always, issues with the environment.

Speaking of the environment, as a way to help stop the Earth from getting pissed and seeking vengeance on us, proceeds from the first two months of sales of Black Bloom will be donated to the Ron Magill Conservation Endowment which is based out of Zoo Miami (www.zoomiami.org/ron-magill-conservation-endowment).

As always, I'd like to acknowledge the people who helped me put this book together: Courtney Swank for her formatting (and reading everything I write), Alessandra Sztrimbely for her helpful edits, and Rosco Nischler for his amazing cover art, constant assistance, and patience. And my brother, Fred, who I dedicate all my work to.

I'd also like to thank you, the reader, for taking this short trip into a bleak future with me. There will be plenty more to come. Stay tuned.

– Dimaro
April 16, 2022

COMING SOON
FROM

2 Novellas
2 Short Stories
1 Horrifying Anthology

Us in Pieces: Stories of Shattered Souls

By Felix I.D. Dimaro

COMING AUGUST 2022

Head over to
www.thingsthatkeepmeupatnight.com for news
and info about upcoming releases from Felix I.D.
Dimaro. And for a preview of Us in Pieces:
Stories of Shattered Souls, you can purchase the
short story "Making Ghosts" on Amazon.